I0761986

BOOKS BY AVA STRONG

REMI LAURENT FBI SUSPENSE THRILLER
THE DEATH CODE (Book #1)
THE MURDER CODE (Book #2)
THE MALICE CODE (Book #3)
THE VENGEANCE CODE (Book #4)
THE DECEPTION CODE (Book #5)
THE SEDUCTION CODE (Book #6)

ILSE BECK FBI SUSPENSE THRILLER
NOT LIKE US (Book #1)
NOT LIKE HE SEEMED (Book #2)
NOT LIKE YESTERDAY (Book #3)
NOT LIKE THIS (Book #4)
NOT LIKE SHE THOUGHT (Book #5)
NOT LIKE BEFORE (Book #6)
NOT LIKE NORMAL (Book #7)

STELLA FALL PSYCHOLOGICAL SUSPENSE THRILLER
HIS OTHER WIFE (Book #1)
HIS OTHER LIE (Book #2)
HIS OTHER SECRET (Book #3)
HIS OTHER MISTRESS (Book #4)
HIS OTHER LIFE (Book #5)
HIS OTHER TRUTH (Book #6)

DAKOTA STEELE FBI SUSPENSE THRILLER
WITHOUT MERCY (Book #1)
WITHOUT REMORSE (Book #2)
WITHOUT A PAST (Book #3)

PROLOGUE

As he walked up the stairs to the front door of the Taylor residence, Steve Todd punched his gloved fist into the opposite hand, whistling through numb lips. It was a freezing January morning, but at least it wasn't snowing, wasn't raining, and in fact the sun was even peeking through the clouds. That meant he could check the Taylor yard off on the maintenance list that always got shorter through the winter months.

He glanced back at the truck idling in the driveway, the exhaust pluming steam into the early morning air. Cocooned in the warmth of the passenger seat, his crew, a.k.a. his son Walter, was in his usual pose, head bowed over his phone. Fingers flying over the keyboard. The youth of today. He was a good enough kid, but didn't want to join his father in the landscaping business. He said it was boring.

Boring it might be, but maintaining the yards of the wealthy folk in the coastal towns of Connecticut was good business. Steve had clients in areas from Bridgeport to Stamford and many in between. This particular home was in Bridgeport.

The Taylors. He'd had a lot of work from them. Redesigned their entire backyard in the years they'd been living here—but Mrs. Taylor was fussy. She was one of those clients who liked to spell everything out. So Steve wasn't allowed to get started without a briefing.

He knocked on the front door and waited. The couple would be up and about by now. They both got off to an early start, which was why he'd gotten here before seven a.m. Both were always rushing out to the office, or meetings, or work conferences. Steve had picked up that they could afford this plush home with its large grounds as a result of their own efforts. Way too many folk in this part of the world seemed to have family money, something that always puzzled Steve, because he, too, was a self-made man who'd grown his business from scratch. He liked knowing he was independent of any family obligations, and could put bread on the table through a hard and honest day's work.

He stamped his feet again, hoping his client would hustle to the door because it was not getting any warmer out here. Maybe he should call. Perhaps Mrs. Taylor was upstairs or around the back, or even already at work, in which case he could hopefully be briefed via a phone call.

Steve dialed her number.

It rang twice. Three times.

As it did, he realized he could hear it from inside the house. Mrs. Taylor's phone was ringing faintly.

It was definitely her phone. The sound had started just after he'd called it, and he recognized the loud, distinctive trill of the ringtone.

"Okay," he said, confused. "Now what?"

Steve didn't know what strange impulse made him try the front door, something he'd never done in the history of his work so far. Barging into someone's home was wrong. It was in fact a surefire way for a landscaper to lose the contract. People didn't appreciate it, particularly in this area where privacy was like a right to most people.

But there was something about that insistent, unanswered ringing that was prickling his senses. And the Taylors were punctual people. They weren't clients who ran late or forgot about appointments.

He turned the handle and, to his shock, the door opened.

Worriedly, he peered into the hallway, with the family room beyond, and the tiled corridor leading to the bedrooms. It all looked in order. Nothing out of place. There hadn't been a fire or a flood or any obvious emergency.

The ringing was louder. It was coming from all the way down the corridor and Steve imagined for a moment that the sound was luring him inside.

"Mrs. Taylor?" he called loudly.

Nothing in reply. No quick footsteps. No shout of "I'll be there in a sec!" Where was she? Had she and her husband had some other crisis and rushed out, and if so, why was her phone inside?

Should he go down the corridor and take a look?

"Uh-uh." He stepped back and closed the door firmly, with hands that were strangely damp. Spooky and strange as this whole situation was, he couldn't just walk into a client's house. He was there to care for their yard. If they came back and found him wandering around inside, he'd be in a shed load of trouble.

But why were they not home?

Scenarios spun through his mind. The less appealing ones were unfortunately top of mind. Had there been a burglary, had the couple fought, had something worse happened?

Perhaps he could look through a window, Steve decided, cutting off his imaginings as they veered toward the gruesome. A window might give him a clue. He was still vaguely uncomfortable with it, but that way at least he'd be able to check if anything was wrong without walking inside their home.

Leaving the front door, he headed around the outside of the house. This was the family room. It had a French door and the curtains were closed. This next room he wasn't sure about. One of the spare bedrooms, perhaps.

If he recalled correctly, the following window was the one in the hall just before the master suite. The main bedroom was higher than the rest of the home, built to accommodate the slope of the land, with a balcony at the far end which looked out onto a formal garden and pond that needed tending year-round.

All the windows beyond this one were above head height, so this was the only possibility.

The curtains were closed but there was a small gap through which Steve peered, his mouth feeling very dry, his spine prickling with uneasiness that he was having to do such a thing.

He hoped beyond hope that there was a reason for this silence and stillness, the unlocked front door and the ringing phone.

Through the tiny gap in the curtains, he could see the colorful splash of a wine-red rug at the bottom of the short staircase leading up to the master suite doorway.

That was it. Just a rug. Nothing else in sight, and nothing untoward.

He shrugged, deciding that he'd have to try and call them later. They wouldn't want him to start without a briefing.

But, as Steve turned away, he rethought what he'd seen.

There had been no rug there last week, he realized, his stomach clenching so violently it was painful. He'd washed the window glass after trimming the grass nearby and he'd only noticed the smooth white tiles. Plus, that rug had been a strange shape. He'd noticed rounded, irregular edges.

Now feeling sick, he returned to the window and this time he craned his neck all the way to the side, trying to see as much as possible of the home's interior.

He gasped in horror as he saw what he'd missed the first time.

It was a foot. A bare foot, jutting into his vision just far enough for him to make out the stark whiteness of the flesh and the strange, darker streaks on the skin.

A cry escaped his mouth, horror and disbelief crowding his mind. This couldn't be! Surely it couldn't be?

A foot, jutting out into a pool of blood?

"Mrs. Taylor? Mr. Taylor?" he shouted loudly through the window, but there was still no response and no movement.

"What the hell?" Steve whispered as the puzzle pieces fitted together in his astounded brain. He didn't know who the foot belonged to, couldn't tell, but it must be one of the Taylors lying there. Where was the spouse, or had something happened to both of them? What catastrophe had played out in this pristine home?

Should he go back inside? Perhaps he could help?

As he hesitated, a voice in the back of his mind told him that would be a very, very bad idea. That what awaited him in there was not just a simple household accident, but something much worse. He feared it was a crime scene.

And the first rule of being around a crime scene, as Steve had learned from the police years ago after stumbling upon a minor incident, was: don't go inside. Don't approach the scene, don't walk in it, don't move anything, don't touch.

Leave it to the investigators, or you open up a world of trouble for yourself.

He decided it would be wise to heed that advice right now.

Feeling sick with dread, he dialed 911 with fingers so unsteady it took him three tries.

Then, as the call connected, his nerve broke. He turned and rushed back toward the warmth and safety of his truck.

"There's been—there's been—something's gone very wrong inside this house!" he gasped to the operator as he stumbled along the path. "I think there must have been a—a death. Or a terrible accident. Please, get here as soon as you can!"

CHAPTER ONE

Stella Fall hurried up the stairs to the meeting room on the hotel's second floor, pushing back her jacket hood, which she'd pulled down low for anonymity as she'd entered the building. She'd tied her long, dark hair back in a braid. Smoothing her hands over it, she checked around her before opening the door.

At this hour, the conference floor of the hotel felt hushed and quiet. It was seven a.m. Not a usual time for meeting in a conference room. But these were not normal circumstances.

The small room—Conference Suite 4—was occupied by one other person, sitting at the far side of the table and watching the door anxiously.

She jumped to her feet as soon as Stella entered, removing the dark glasses she'd been wearing.

"Viv!" Stella greeted the tall, slender blonde.

"Stella Fall. It's been a while. Thanks for getting here early."

"It's no problem. I'm used to early mornings now that I'm with the FBI," Stella explained. Her alarm clock was usually set for six a.m., and she'd either head straight to work, or to the gym and then to work, depending on her caseload.

As Viv walked around the table to give her a hug, Stella felt a sense of unreality that she was reconnecting with somebody that she'd first met during her short and disastrous stay with the Marshall family.

Back then, Viv, who'd divorced one of the Marshalls years ago, had been introduced as a family friend. Blond, beautiful, and self-assured, Stella had perceived her as one of that elite clan. Although divorced, she was still part of their inner circle—mostly because she knew their secrets.

Now, as she gave Stella an awkward embrace, Stella was shocked by how she'd changed in the eight months since they'd last seen each other. She'd lost weight and looked stressed. Her face was gaunt, her cheekbones sharply defined. Her skin looked pale and dull. With no make-up, the black coat she wore seemed to leach all the color from her face. Only her blue eyes were as sharp and piercing as Stella remembered them.

"I'm so sorry about what's happened," Stella said.

Viv nodded. "It hasn't been great," she admitted, and Stella was sure she was thinking back on the chain of events that had led up to this moment.

When Stella had been a murder suspect, estranged from her fiancé's family and in the worst predicament of her life, Viv had been the one who'd first hinted about the Marshalls' misdoings, their corrupt and illegal activities, and that their closet was crammed with skeletons.

Stella had told the police, and since then, the Marshalls had been fighting a desperate battle against multiple charges. Ex-senator Gordon Marshall blamed Stella for everything, most recently his wife's tragic suicide. But in his search for scapegoats, he now suspected Viv had betrayed the family.

Stella knew Viv was in serious danger.

"Where are you staying? You need to go into hiding," she said, wanting to get to the most important part of the meeting—for her, anyway—which was to ensure Viv's safety. Stella wasn't powerless in this regard. She was now an FBI special agent. She could help Viv. She could organize for her to go into a safe house.

But it was clear that Viv didn't want that. Even as Stella spoke, she was shaking her head.

"No. I can't hide forever and I'm not going to. I'm back at home but I'm being careful. I've tightened up on security. I've changed the locks. Installed motion-sensor lights. Put a security door in the corridor leading to my bedroom."

Stella shook her head, feeling tension coil inside her again. "It's not enough, Viv. It won't be enough."

"I hid away for the charity event, as you advised. I felt terrible about doing it. As if I was letting everyone down. I felt like I was letting my fears get the better of me. I can't live my life that way."

"You need to lay low for a while," Stella entreated, wishing that Viv wasn't such a strong, brave person, because right now, fear would keep her safer.

They'd already come after Stella. They hadn't succeeded, but Stella still woke, screaming, from nightmares following the attack. An anonymous man had tried to strangle her while she was on a case, and had almost succeeded. If her case partner hadn't heard her kicking the wall and burst into her room, she would have died.

And a few days ago, Stella had read about a body discovered on the Greenwich coast, shot three times in the chest. The man—mid-thirties, fit, five-nine—had been in possession of a false ID and his real identity had been linked back to a number of serious crimes.

Stella was sure he'd been the hit man who'd attacked her a few weeks ago. He was the same height and build. And now he was dead. That scared her. Who had killed him? Who would they hire next? There was no limit to the Marshalls' capacity for revenge.

"I won't need to lay low for much longer," Viv said firmly. She smiled at Stella and for a moment, when her face lit up, she looked more like the woman Stella remembered.

"What do you mean?" Stella lowered her voice, scooting her chair closer to Viv's. Over the smell of carpets and furniture polish in this slightly stuffy room, Stella picked up the faint floral scent of Viv's shampoo.

"I've been doing my own investigation," Viv told her in a whisper. "I hired a top private investigator from out of state. He's been working for the past couple of weeks. He's been able to access phone calls, track movements, follow some financial transactions, even record a couple of conversations. He's uncovered a lot of evidence so far linking them to the hit man, and other recent crimes also."

"Seriously?" Stella felt breathless with hope that finally, the Marshalls might be crushed for good.

"Gordon Marshall and Cecilia's sister, Kathy, will both be heavily implicated." Viv dropped her voice even lower, breathing the next words. "I told him I need all the evidence. I need this to be rock-solid. I can't afford for it to break apart. I need Gordon to be jailed, and bail denied, after he's arrested. Which will be soon," she added, sounding confident.

"I still think you need to go into hiding until the arrest is made."

Viv shook her head. "It won't take long. As soon as I have what I need, I'm going to take it to the police immediately. That's what I wanted to tell you, Stella. What the Marshalls have done is going to backfire on them. I'm going to make sure of it."

"Please, please let me get you somewhere safe. Just for two days," Stella begged.

Viv shook her head. "I don't want them to know I'm scared, or hiding," she explained. "There's still one piece of evidence this investigator is obtaining. I don't want them to get a heads-up something's wrong, or he might not be able to get it."

"Can you ask a cop to stay with you?" she asked, knowing that Viv didn't trust private security as the Marshalls had links with the local firms.

Viv smiled ruefully. "With what cause? I've had no direct threats on my life. Now I must ask an overworked policeman to drop what he's doing and come and guard me twenty-four hours a day in my already highly secure home? What do you think they'll say? They'll tell me to go get private security and stop wasting police resources."

Stella shook her head, acknowledging Viv's argument. As a stubborn person herself, she knew when she was up against the same quality in others. Viv wasn't going to budge. She hoped nothing would go wrong in this short but critical timeframe.

"Let me know if there's anything I can do to help," she said.

"I will. This will all be over soon, I promise you. We're going to deal them a blow they can't come back from," Viv told her, her voice strong and assured.

*

As she drove back to her apartment after the meeting, Stella felt hopeful, but also seriously worried. She hated that Viv was putting herself so badly at risk, even if she was being defiant in the face of danger. And she hated even more that Viv had to expose herself to potential harm, just to try and save herself and Stella.

How was it possible that the toxic, evil, and corrupt Marshalls were not all already in jail?

Stella drove into her apartment's basement parking garage, where she'd recently booked a bay. Now that it was winter, she needed to be ready to head to the office at a moment's notice, and couldn't afford to spend time scraping ice from the windshield or demisting the window glass.

At any rate, that was what Stella told herself, even though she knew the real reason was that having her car parked in a secure basement felt safer than being out on the street. She could drive inside and get out of her car knowing she wasn't being watched.

But not this time.

After this meeting, her senses were on the highest alert. It was because she was looking closely at her surroundings that she spotted the person standing in a dark corner of the basement.

The figure was dressed in dark jeans and a black hooded jacket, very similar to the gear she'd chosen for the meeting with Viv.

There was something about the way this person was lurking out of sight, in the already gloomy basement, and the way their head turned instantly as they clocked Stella's car and number plate, that got all her nerves jangling.

Hitting the brakes and taking a closer look, she couldn't see anything. Whoever was standing there had retreated out of sight behind the pillar.

She would have reversed straight out again, but the automated boom had already lowered. Panic surged inside her as she remembered that life-and-death struggle with the killer.

She had her gun with her, belted under her jacket. It was uncomfortable when she drove, but she didn't mind. The discomfort of having it dig into her was more than worth the reassurance of knowing that her weapon was within easy reach.

Stella accelerated through the basement, deciding to drive straight to the exit and get away. She flinched at the looming shadows cast by her headlights. Sick fear welled inside her. She hated feeling powerless and vulnerable, even though she knew that so soon after a nearly-fatal attack this was inevitable.

At the last minute, she changed her mind. She was not going to head out of the basement. She was going to face this person, whoever it was, and confront them.

Wrenching the wheel to the side, she spun the car into her bay. She pushed the door open and leaped out, grabbing her gun from the holster as she ran to where she'd seen the lurking figure.

But the watcher had gone.

Only shadows remained. With hands that felt cold and shaky, Stella took her phone out and activated the flashlight, banishing the darkness.

Had she imagined this? For a moment she doubted what she'd seen. Perhaps she'd been so spooked after the meeting with Viv that her mind had conjured this up.

But then she saw the evidence. It was a partial footprint, because the person must have stood in the shallow puddle that had blown in through a ventilation grate.

Using her phone, Stella photographed the footprint. The person had been wearing trainers with a distinctive pattern on the sole. There was no heel print, so she couldn't tell the size. But it was clear proof that someone had been standing here and had vanished as soon as they'd been noticed.

She had no idea who they were. But she feared that this was just the start. They were in her home territory, watching and waiting. She had to watch her back even more carefully now, because the threats against her were only going to stop when Gordon Marshall was in jail for life, or she was dead.

Her phone buzzed in her hand and she jumped, realizing how wound up she was. Checking it, her heart quickening, she saw a text from Roth.

"We have a new murder case just called in. I'm assigning you to it. Please come in asap for your briefing," it read.

CHAPTER TWO

Stella rushed into the New Haven FBI offices, feeling as if the pressure was intensifying from all directions. At the same time, she was relieved to have a case to focus on.

She felt the familiar thrill of nervousness and excitement at the thought of what would be waiting. What case would it be? What had happened?

And even more importantly, who would she be partnered with?

Both she and Special Agent Rick Maxwell had requested that Roth partner them together for the next case. She felt ready to join up with Maxwell again, for work at least, though not for the budding romance that had caused such a disaster between them. She was steering clear of that. Maybe forever, but at least until his pathologically jealous ex-wife was firmly out of the picture.

But would Roth choose Maxwell? He might have other ideas. Stella could be partnered with somebody new, or even with her erstwhile rival, Carrie Potts.

She was surprised to realize that she wouldn't mind if she was partnered with Carrie again. Their last investigation had taught her a lot about overcoming differences. When finding a killer was at stake, personal issues had to be put aside or the case suffered. And when they were put aside, it was surprising how easy it was to find common ground.

Every crime investigation felt like a personal challenge to Stella. She felt a burning desire to find the killer, to see justice done, to make the offender pay for the wrongs that he or she had committed.

Inside the office, she greeted the attendant at the security checkpoint with a smile. The first time she'd walked into this sleek, multi-story building, she'd felt intimidated by its size and scale and by the mere fact she was working with the FBI. Now, her workplace felt familiar and even friendly.

She hustled down the corridor, eager to find out the details on her latest case.

Walking into Roth's office, she immediately picked up the rich aroma of coffee, the fuel that powered her boss's seemingly limitless energy.

The tousle-haired Roth was heading into the meeting room, carrying a tray with three cups. He turned and nodded a quick greeting when he saw her.

"Fall. Come on in."

Stella felt butterflies surge inside her. She hadn't felt so nervous for ages. Who would her partner be? What was this case about?

Entering, she suppressed a relieved grin as she saw Maxwell sitting on the far side of the meeting table.

"Maxwell!" she said.

"Fall." The fit, dark-haired Maxwell met her gaze and she saw the same relief in his eyes. Perhaps he also hadn't known who his partner would be until she'd arrived. Maxwell was clearly amped to be working with her again.

"We have an urgent case in Bridgeport. Double homicide."

He passed the coffee cups around but nobody stirred or drank. Both she and Maxwell were fixed on Roth's words and the meeting room felt strangely silent.

"The landscaper arrived this morning and called nine-one-one when he realized something was wrong. The victims are Mr. and Mrs. Taylor. They were murdered in their home, probably late last night. Forensics are still busy, and it's a bloody scene, I believe, so they will be there awhile."

Stella felt, rather than saw, Maxwell's concerned glance in her direction.

"Do they know what happened?" she asked.

"They are still piecing it together," Roth said, and her palms turned icy cold as he continued. "There are some characteristics that point to it being a possible serial killer case, which is why we've been involved immediately. The husband was tortured before his death."

A serial killer? Stella's heart sped up.

No cases were more difficult to solve. The victim might be chosen just because he or she suited the killer's devious agenda, and there were often no clear ties to the killer.

If this was a serial, it was going to be her toughest case yet, and Roth was clearly under pressure with it.

"We need fast results with this one," her boss continued. "Cases like this generate a huge amount of fear. We need answers, we need an arrest, and whoever is doing this, we can't let it happen again."

He glanced down at his coffee cup as if he'd forgotten all about it. Then he drained the contents. Thinking she might need a shot of caffeine, Stella did the same.

"There's no more I can tell you, so get going as soon as you can," Roth said. "I'm leaving for a day of meetings just now. I'll have to travel to Washington at some stage today, so this is in your hands. Brief me on your progress when you get a gap."

"Will do." Stella stood up and walked out of the room, with Maxwell following close behind her.

Stella's thoughts were deeply troubled as they walked to the car in silence. A serial killer case. This would be the first of its kind that she was handling. The thought of going up against a true psychopath was challenging and scary. Especially since she'd learned that her father had been involved in a similar case when he'd disappeared all those years ago.

Maxwell let out a deep breath as they headed out of the parking lot.

"This is going to be a tough one," he said, the brief summary echoing all of Stella's fears.

"It is," she agreed.

"I'm glad I'm partnered with you on this," Maxwell continued as he drove onto the main road. "This was your thesis topic, wasn't it? Serial killers and their mentality?"

Stella felt a flash of pleasure that Maxwell had remembered.

"Yes."

Traffic going out of town was moving freely compared to the long tailbacks on the way in. Speeding along the main road, Stella tried to prepare herself mentally for what would be her first serial case. She thought back over her thesis and the interviews she'd done with imprisoned serial murderers.

It was going to be important, but challenging, to try and get into the killer's mind. Although serial murders appeared illogical, there was usually a twisted logic to their actions. They were violent, antisocial people who laughed at society's norms, and yet, they were usually cunning enough to hide undetected within society, taking on a cloak of normality.

Wrapped in her thoughts, Stella was surprised to see they were already approaching Parkway Drive, where the Taylors' home was located. Maxwell turned onto the winding, tree-lined avenue, and then hit the brakes as he saw the scene up ahead.

The large home was surrounded by flashing lights, and a multitude of vehicles were parked on the sidewalk and in the street. Police and emergency services were there, together with two SUVs from a local security firm. Word must have spread, because there were other cars outside as well. Neighbors and bystanders were clustered around, swaddled in dark jackets and warm hats. They stood well back from the double strand of yellow crime scene tape that fluttered in the breeze.

Two people with cameras—a young, blond woman and a bearded man, stood on the highest part of the sidewalk straining for a view of the home's front door. The press was here. Already, this case was attracting media attention.

"Where can we park?" Maxwell muttered.

Stella pointed to the opposite side of the road.

"Maybe there?"

He nodded. He drove up onto the grass and they climbed out.

The wind cut through Stella as they hurried across the road. The tape flapped and rattled as they raised it and walked underneath.

Clearly not trusting the tape alone to keep the worried crowds back, a police detective was standing guard. He turned to them as soon as they lifted the tape, taking a warning step in their direction.

"FBI," Maxwell said, quickly showing his badge, and the detective nodded, looking relieved.

"Go on," he said. "Detective in charge is Grant. He'll brief you."

Stella felt relieved that the name was familiar. She had worked with Detective Grant before, on a murder case in Fairfield. There he was—a short, balding man with a good-natured face that currently looked stressed and harassed. Standing at the front door, he was speaking urgently on a phone held in one of his gloved hands.

He glanced up and saw them.

"FBI is here. I'll call you back," he said.

He turned to them.

"Maxwell. Fall. Good to see you. Glad you got here so quick," he said.

"Where shall we start?" Stella asked.

Grant thought for a moment, glancing at the crowds outside.

"Forensics are still at work in the back section of the home. It's a mess."

Maxwell nodded. “Best to let them finish. We don’t need to view the scene yet, if you can talk us through it.”

“Okay. Come inside. The family room and kitchen have been checked. They were clean, no trace or prints to be found. It seems everything happened down the corridor. Just put on foot covers in case. Let’s talk in the kitchen and I can update you.”

Stella was already shivering. She felt glad to step inside the large, luxurious home, even though it didn’t feel like a comforting place with the buzz of voices, occasional shouts, thumping of footsteps from down the passage. Quickly, they pulled on foot covers and headed inside.

The Taylors’ home was large and unapologetically modern, Stella saw. No nod to New England heritage in this bright, streamlined home. The white-tiled hallway was stark and pristine, with two paintings providing a splash of color. As she bent to adjust one of the foot covers, she felt warmth radiating from the under-floor heating below the granite tiles.

They headed down a short corridor. Along the way, a wide archway opened into a large entertainment area on the left leading out to a pool.

Beyond that, another archway led to a more formal living room on the right, and opposite that, an open door led through to the kitchen. It was well equipped with gleaming, ultra-luxury appliances and looked pristine.

“What do you have so far?” Stella asked as they walked inside.

“The residents, Mark and Diane Taylor, were murdered last night. We’re still working on the timeframe. Probably between nine and eleven p.m. The home had a state-of-the-art security system but it was disabled. The killer might have gained entry through the window in the entertainment area. It looks as if the latch is not functioning correctly and it could have been pushed inward.”

“And the security system? How was that disabled?” Stella asked.

Grant shrugged. “All we can say is that it is working. So either it was never turned on, or it was deactivated by someone, or it was bypassed in some other way.”

Stella nodded. The alarm could have been turned off by the home owners themselves. Hearing a sound, the husband might have decided to go and investigate. Especially in a seemingly safe neighborhood, nobody really thought a psychopathic killer would be waiting. Perhaps they had thought a window had been left open and was banging in the wind, or the neighbors’ cat had strayed inside. She could imagine the conversation that might have played out.

"What is that noise?"

"I don't know, honey. Let me go see."

"What if it's a burglar? Shouldn't we call security?"

"I'm sure it isn't. But I'll take a golf club with me."

"Were they in bed at the time? What was the sequence of events?" Stella asked.

"From what we can see, Mark Taylor came face to face with the killer in the corridor outside the master bedroom. Mark was wearing a robe."

Stella nodded. So he probably had been in bed, and was alerted by a noise.

"We think he must have been knocked out, or at any rate, stunned. He has a wound on the top of his head that doesn't seem to be caused by a fall. There's a short staircase leading up to the master bedroom—five stairs, with a wrought-iron railing. The killer tied his hands to the stair rail and gagged him, using the belt from his robe."

"Then what?" Maxwell's voice also sounded more unsteady than usual. Stella guessed that with less than two years' experience in the FBI so far, this was his first case of this nature, too.

"Then we think he went into the bedroom. I'm saying 'he' because of the strength that was clearly used in this attack. We can't rule out that it might also have been a strong woman, but a man is more likely. It could have been more than one person, but there is only one set of footprints visible," Grant explained as Stella nodded.

"He must have worked fast, or quietly, because Diane Taylor was still in bed," Grant continued. "That's why we are assuming that he went there right away. Disabled Mark, and headed straight through to Diane. He surprised her and it looks as if he basically beat her to death, quickly and efficiently, using whatever he used to stun Mark," he said.

"Any idea about the weapon?" Maxwell said.

"Possibly a baseball bat, or something similar. He must have taken it with him when he was done. There's no evidence of a weapon in the home, although we haven't finished searching the yard," Grant explained.

"Then what happened?" Stella asked.

"Then the killer returned to the husband. He took his time with him, and he used a knife," Grant said. "The corridor is a bloodbath. Coroner's guess is that he eventually bled out. None of the cuts were deep enough or placed correctly to kill him on their own."

Stella wondered if the non-lethal cuts had been intentional, designed to prolong the victim's agony. That would point toward an ice-cold psychopath with some experience or knowledge.

But again there was also the chance that the attacker had been angry, stabbing and cutting, but had not struck deep or hard enough to kill. So there were two alternate scenarios to consider. One was a serial murderer. The other was an angry person, or people, who hadn't had the will or expertise to inflict a fatal stab wound.

"Is there any trace evidence so far? What about those footprints?" Stella asked. In such a grim, bloody scene the chance of trace would be high. But to her shock, Grant shook his head, looking frustrated.

"We've found nothing so far, but we haven't finished searching the scene yet. The footprints don't make sense. They're overly large and shapeless. We think he could have stuck something on the bottom of his shoes to disguise their size and tread."

"Preplanning," Stella observed.

"This was a well-researched crime, without a doubt," Grant said heavily. "Not random. Nobody gets so lucky doing things on impulse."

He rubbed his forehead with one of his gloved hands, as if trying to ease a throbbing headache. Stella felt sympathy for him, and at the same time, she was scared by what they were up against.

"Was anything stolen?" Stella asked.

"Not that we can see. Both their phones were still in the bedroom and we've already sent them through to the technicians to be unlocked."

"What did Mark and Diane do for a living?" she asked, wondering if this crime could be related to their work if one of them had a high-risk job.

"Both worked full-time. They had no children. Mark is thirty-eight, and he was one of the partners in an accounting firm. Diane is thirty-six, and she was a marketing director for a cosmetics firm. We've already made contact with both their workplaces, but nothing is ringing alarm bells in that direction."

"What about their families?" Stella asked, thinking immediately of the tensions that could run deep and destructive within a family.

"We asked the secretary at Diane's work, who knew her quite well, for contact details. It turns out they don't have any close family members in Connecticut. Diane is an only child and her parents live in San Francisco, and she thinks Mark's parents moved to Kenya, or at any rate somewhere in Africa, a few years ago."

"Who found the bodies? Is that person cleared of any involvement?"

Grant nodded. "Yes. The man who found the bodies was the owner of the landscaping firm the Taylors used. He didn't go into the home at all. Apparently he caught sight of one of the bodies through a window, got a serious fright, and called us right away. His movements last night and this morning are accounted for. Last night he was with his wife and two kids at their home in Torrington. They watched movies until ten. This morning, he dropped his younger child at the local high school on the way to the Taylors', and stopped for coffee and gas at his local gas station."

Stella turned to look at Maxwell, who was frowning slightly. She knew the expression meant he was thinking hard, theorizing on the best course of action, just as she was doing.

"We need to look into their personal lives closely," Maxwell said.

Remembering her earlier thoughts about the possibility of a pattern, Stella said, "I'd also like to check for any other similar crimes, going back a few years. In the wider area, not necessarily in this precinct only. Any husband-and-wife or couple murders that followed a similar pattern."

Grant nodded somberly. "We can do that. I'll ask our detectives to look back in our records and contact the other precincts statewide."

Anxiety clenched inside Stella. There already seemed to be a notable lack of evidence in all directions. But perhaps someone nearby had seen something, even if they didn't realize what they had seen.

Across the street, she could see the front door of the home was open and a gray-haired man was peering anxiously out.

"Let's speak to the neighbors first," she said.

CHAPTER THREE

Stella headed out into the fresh, gusty morning, and she and Maxwell strode purposefully across the road.

This home had a sweeping front yard that was neatly maintained, with rose bushes that were now stubby and pruned back, and hedges that were impeccably trimmed.

The gray-haired man stepped out of the house and made his way toward them, looking nervous and unsure. He was wearing a fleece jacket and tracksuit pants. This combination on a working day made Stella think he might be retired. She guessed he was in his mid-sixties.

"FBI agents Fall and Maxwell," Stella introduced. "Sir, we need to speak to you."

"Of course," he replied, sounding courteous, but with a clear undertone of worry in his voice. "I'm Graham Haddow. Please, I understand if you can't give any details, but tell me—are Mark and Diane okay?"

Stella saw his hands were trembling slightly.

"No, Mr. Haddow," Maxwell said regretfully. "I'm sorry to say they have both been murdered."

Graham closed his eyes briefly and put his hands over his face. He stayed like that for a while before lowering his hands, which were shaking more badly now. He gazed at the agents in shock.

"This is unbelievable. I literally cannot take this in. It's like a nightmare. They were friends. Good people. Good neighbors. Please—do you mind? I need to sit."

He turned and stumbled inside. Stella and Maxwell followed him as he headed into a well-furnished living room. He slumped down onto a blue leather couch as abruptly as if his legs had been knocked out from under him. Breathing rapidly, he leaned forward, staring at the floor.

Stella gave Maxwell a worried glance. She hoped the shock had not seriously affected this man.

"Are you feeling all right? Can I bring you a glass of water? A cup of tea?" Stella glanced toward where she thought the kitchen must be.

He raised his head. His face looked very pale.

"No. I'm okay. This is just such a shock." He stared at her, and she saw a surprising kindness in his pale blue eyes. "But you're the ones we should be worrying about now. Our detectives and first responders. Are you okay? Can I make you some tea?" He scrambled shakily to his feet.

Stella felt touched by his empathy at such a stressful time. She also felt encouraged by his concern for them, because concerned neighbors knew more about what was happening in their area. They were more observant and sensitive. They looked out for others around them. It could well be that this frail-looking man held important information, even if he didn't know it yet.

"Thank you for the offer, but please, sit down," Stella said gently as Graham lowered himself onto his seat again.

"In terms of the crime, police are still piecing together what happened," she said, deciding it would be better to give no further information at this time.

"What were your movements last night, Mr. Haddow?" Maxwell said. Stella knew this question would serve to check the man's alibi, but also confirm if he might have seen or heard anything.

"I went out to eat at a restaurant in the center on the beachfront. Beachview, I think it's called. The center, I mean. The restaurant is called Amigos. It's my Tuesday night routine, as they do a deal on seafood, which I love."

"What time did you get back?" Maxwell asked.

"About half past nine. I sat at the restaurant and read my book, and then I took a cab home, as I had two beers with my meal," Graham said.

Coming home at that hour meant he could have seen or heard something.

"Did you notice anything unusual?" Stella asked. "Any vehicles nearby? Any activity across the road? Were the lights on?"

Pressing his lips together, Graham was thinking hard. But then he gave a defeated sigh.

"I don't recall anything. When I take a cab, I always go inside as fast as possible because the drivers generally wait to see if I'm in safe. Which, given what happened yesterday, is just as well. I wish now that I had stopped and looked."

"Did you hear anything when you were home?" she asked.

Graham shook his head. "I had a shower and got into bed, where I watched television for about an hour. Then I went to sleep. I didn't hear a thing, but I have been suspecting for a while that I am going slightly deaf. I have been turning the television up higher than I used to. I wish now I had chosen differently. If I'd been reading, perhaps I might have heard something."

Stella nodded, feeling disappointed.

"Do you think we neighbors are in any danger?" Graham asked. "When I was standing outside earlier, some people were saying they thought it was a violent robbery gone wrong. I'm worried about that. Is there anything I should do in terms of security? Have there been any other cases in the area?"

"Nothing like this has happened in this neighborhood. But it's a good idea to be extra cautious for the next while," Stella said.

"Did you know the Taylors well? Were you good friends?" Maxwell asked.

Graham nodded. "They were very good neighbors. I moved here a few years ago after my wife passed away, and they were immediately friendly. They invited me for dinner regularly, every month or two. They would often bring me extra if they'd ordered craft beer or cookies or anything that could be shared. They both worked very hard."

"Tell me about that?" Stella asked.

"They were real career-focused people. They worked long hours, but when they were not working, they were sociable. I'd sometimes see their friends parked outside on weekends. But they didn't throw big parties. They were not excessive people. Quiet."

"When you visited them, did you ever pick up on anything that was wrong?" Stella asked. This was an important question and she hoped that Graham would be able to recall these details.

"Like what?" he said, sounding confused.

"Any fights. Any problems. Any issues with family or friends or people in the area?"

Graham thought for a moment.

"No," he said, sounding apologetic. "I didn't pick up on that at all. They never seemed like they were bothered about any big issues. They didn't seem to have any problems with others. Nothing was obvious to me anyway."

"Did you ever hear anything unusual?" she asked, remembering that Graham was a little deaf but deciding to give the question a try anyway. "Any shouts, fights? Either of them storming out? Any of their other guests leaving in a rage, revving the car, anything like that?"

Again, Graham considered her words carefully before replying in a regretful voice.

"Nothing like that. I'm here a lot of the time, but I am across the road from them and as I say, slightly deaf. I definitely don't recall any fights, but the neighbors to their right, the Parsons, might know more. They have kids and I believe Anthea, the wife, is a stay-at-home parent. They're lovely people, also very kind and neighborly, so might well have seen or heard something."

"We'll speak to them next," Stella said. "You've been very helpful. We may need to get more information from you later."

"Sure. Of course. You can speak to me any time. Here's my number." Graham reached over to the side table and picked up a notepad where he scribbled it down. He ripped out the page and handed it to Stella.

Then he stared at her and Maxwell, looking serious and intent.

"I can't believe this has happened. It's left me feeling afraid, to the extent that I don't think I want to live here anymore. I've lost two good friends and I've lost the feeling of safety I had here. Please, Agents, if there is anything I can help you with, contact me. At any time. I'll keep my phone with me. Whatever it takes, I want to get closure on this."

Stella thanked him again.

She hoped that with one of them being a stay-at-home parent, the neighbors to the right of the Taylors might have seen or heard something important. Walking out of Graham's home, she headed in their direction.

CHAPTER FOUR

As Maxwell left Graham Haddow's home, he looked around him, noting that scattered groups of onlookers and emergency services were still on the scene. The community was severely shaken by this. People were anxiously watching as he and Fall headed for the street.

The morning had been so busy that he hadn't had a chance to speak to Fall about another issue that was worrying him deeply.

It involved Brigitte, his ex-wife.

As they headed across the road, approaching the Taylors' righthand neighbors, Maxwell felt tension knot inside him. He'd spoken to Brigitte on the weekend. As gently as he could, he had broken the news that for him, the marriage was over. That he was not prepared to try again and that he was going to start divorce proceedings.

She'd taken it even worse than he'd expected. Brigitte had exploded with rage. And as he'd feared, she had immediately suspected that there was someone else in his life, and accused him that he was doing this because he wanted to be together with another woman.

"Who is it? Tell me who this whore is who's stolen you from me! This was never meant to happen between us!" she'd threatened. Then, when he'd said nothing, she'd started casting around for ideas.

"Was it that dark-haired bitch who's your work partner? What's her name? Stella Fall? Because now I think about it, Maxwell, you mentioned her a lot. Is she more than just a colleague? Has she been trying to steal you? I won't stand for that! I won't!"

He felt his blood pressure spike as he remembered the argument, which had lasted for hours, and how Brigitte had repeatedly lost it with him, screaming and threatening. She'd showed him all the anger, rage, and insecurity that were usually buried deep within her damaged psyche.

With her demons unleashed, he dreaded what she might do to Fall. Brigitte was sly, and once she had an idea in her head, there was no dislodging it. If she'd turned the full force of her pathological jealousy onto Fall, Maxwell feared there would be consequences. She would find out where Fall lived. She would research it and follow the clues.

Maxwell knew Fall was as tough as nails, and more than capable of defending herself, but he didn't want her to have to do that. She was under enough stress with the Marshalls. She didn't need more threats and worries in her life, and especially not while Maxwell was trying to mend the damage that he had done.

He could get a restraining order, he thought, as they headed up the paved garden path to the neighbor's house. The problem was that you couldn't obtain such a thing without a reason. Until Brigitte made her move, he couldn't use that option. But once she'd made the move, it might be too late.

He knew he should warn Fall, but that would also open a can of worms, especially since they'd only just gotten back to their original footing and were partnered together again. Maxwell did not want to bring up the issues with his ex-wife, which had caused the disaster in the first place.

Returning his full focus to the case and trying to suppress his worry, Maxwell knocked on the white-painted front door.

A moment later, it was opened just a crack by a strawberry blonde who peeked nervously through the gap.

"FBI," Fall said, stepping forward and speaking in reassuring tones to the clearly frightened woman as she showed her badge.

"FBI?" the woman repeated, sounding even more nervous. After a short pause, she opened the door wider. "Rog?" she called to someone out of Maxwell's sight. "The FBI is here."

"I'm on my way."

A moment later, a tall, mustached man hurried into the hallway. He was dressed in motorbike leathers and looked just as worried as his wife.

"Hi. I'm Roger Parsons. This is Anthea, my wife. What's the story here, and what do you want from us?" Roger asked. He sounded scared, rather than guilty, Maxwell thought, but reminded himself not to assume that anyone was innocent yet.

"We're gathering information on this crime. May we speak inside?" Fall asked, in that soothing tone that had the strawberry blonde stepping aside to let them in before she'd even realized what she was doing.

"Sure," Anthea said. "We don't even know what happened. The police told us there was a murder. We're really disturbed by this. We're all holed up here until we know it's safe."

"Mr. and Mrs. Taylor were both killed. We don't know the full circumstances yet, but we're working on it," Maxwell said, wishing there was an easier way to give this news to people who knew the victims. It never seemed to get easier.

Anthea clapped her hands over her mouth, tears welling in her eyes. She turned to her husband, who put his arm protectively around her shoulders, rubbing them as he guided her inside.

"I don't—I don't believe this! Both our neighbors? Both of them?" Anthea repeated, sounding utterly shocked as she stumbled alongside him.

Maxwell followed Fall into the home. Though spacious and luxuriously furnished, this was most definitely a family home, rather than the showpiece houses that he so often saw. Three school bags were lined up at the foot of the stairs, and a toy horse with a lime green mane was lying on the hall table. The decorative crystal dish on the table was filled with marbles and small model dinosaurs.

Roger led the way into the family room. "Please sit," he said.

Maxwell sat down on the leather sofa, noting a plethora of juice glasses and plates on the dining room table in this open-plan living space.

"I'm sorry. The place is a mess," Roger explained. "Our housekeeper would usually be in today but we told her to stay away, as I wasn't sure what was happening or how safe it was. I stayed home from work and we've kept the kids home from school. My sister's fetching them, and we're going to let them sleep with her for a few nights. We're scared for their safety and for ours. I mean, we could be next, right?"

He sat down in one of the armchairs after moving a discarded doll aside. Maxwell noticed his jacket was embroidered with a badge: "Roger Parsons Bikes, Spares & Service." So he owned his business.

"At this stage, we don't know what the motive for the murders is," Maxwell explained, realizing that his words would bring this anxious couple little comfort. "So yes, keep your family as safe as possible and take all precautions."

"What happened?" Anthea stared at them anxiously.

Maxwell glanced at Fall. He wasn't up to disclosing the gory details.

"An intruder, or intruders, gained access to the home and murdered both Mr. and Mrs. Taylor last night," Stella said.

Maxwell knew she didn't want them to know that the killer had probably been in the home for over an hour, and that Mark's death had not been quick. He felt sickened again at the level of sadism it would take to do such a thing.

"I didn't hear a gunshot," Roger insisted, with a note of challenge in his voice. "And I was up from about ten until after midnight with our youngest. This is a quiet neighborhood. Surely I would have heard something? When did this happen?"

"We can't give more details until the postmortem is completed," Fall said firmly, to Maxwell's relief. "But neither of them was shot, so you didn't miss a gunshot."

Maxwell saw the couple exchange appalled glances. He knew they were mentally recalibrating their theories of what might have happened, and coming up with an even more violent conclusion.

"If you were awake at that time, did you hear or see anything else? Any noises? A car arriving or departing?" Fall continued.

"No, I heard nothing," Roger said, sounding frustrated. "The kids sleep in the bedroom next to ours, and those are both on the opposite side of the house from the Taylors."

"I was out for the count," Anthea said apologetically. "I had about two hours' sleep on the weekend, which is why Roger helped me last night. I was in bed by eight, and only woke at five this morning."

Maxwell knew there was potentially the opportunity for the husband to have sneaked out and committed the murder himself. It was unlikely but to rule it out completely, he needed to dig further into the relationship between these two families.

"Did you know the Taylors well?" he asked.

"Not very well. We would always greet each other, and have a chat, but we didn't socialize. They worked very long hours and were both very focused on their careers, while we're so occupied with the kids."

Stella felt disappointed. She'd hoped for more close contact between the Taylors and these neighbors.

"Our socializing consists mostly of talking to other parents at their children's parties," Anthea said. "They were very friendly though. Good neighbors. On the odd occasion that we needed to organize things with them, like chopping a tree branch or having the plumbers gain access to fix a pipe, it was never a problem and vice versa."

"I know they were friendly with Graham across the road," Roger said.

At that, Anthea hissed in a shocked breath, so suddenly that everyone turned to her in concern.

"Graham! I hadn't even thought about him. Do you know, is he okay?"

"He's fine, ma'am. Very disturbed by this, just as you are. We've just been interviewing him."

Anthea sighed in relief. "We should check in on him. He must be terribly upset by this and is probably feeling as unsafe as we are."

"Good idea." Roger nodded. "I need to speak to him about upgrading our neighborhood security also. Maybe installing street cameras. He's on the board of our local residents' association and can hopefully push for them. We don't have cameras at present, unfortunately, as nobody thought there would be a need for them," he told Stella and Maxwell.

The lack of cameras was a blow. They would have provided valuable information, Maxwell knew.

"That depends whether we stay here. I think we should move," Anthea insisted. "I don't feel comfortable living here after something so violent happened next door."

"When was the last time you spoke to the Taylors?" Maxwell asked.

"Friday evening. We were arriving home from a school meeting and saw them heading out. I guess that would have been at about half past seven?" Anthea said.

Roger nodded. "Yes. About that time. Mark and I spoke through our windows, made a few jokes about the weather, which was sleety and awful. Then they drove off, and we drove inside."

This confirmed to Maxwell that there was no animosity and that the relationship had been good and neighborly.

"When will we find out more?" Anthea asked. "We really need to make decisions."

Maxwell gave her a sympathetic glance.

"This case is a top priority. We are going to be working pretty much around the clock until we find the killer," he said.

Fall raised an eyebrow at Maxwell and he gave a tiny shake of his head. The unspoken question was whether there was anything else they needed to ask these people and the answer was no. Maxwell liked it that their level of communication was so subtle and easy. He'd missed it in the past few weeks.

They both stood up.

“Thanks for your time,” Maxwell said. “If there’s anything you think of, or remember, please call immediately.” He handed Roger one of his cards.

As they headed to the door, Maxwell thought back again to that tiny moment of unspoken communication, and realized how much it meant to him. He felt amped about being partnered with Stella again. Together, he was sure they had the best chance of solving this crime.

But Maxwell knew he had to do more than solve the case. He also had to make sure that his pathologically jealous ex-wife did not end up harming Fall.

“Shall we go next door and see if forensics has finished up?” she asked him.

“Sure,” Maxwell said, once again shelving his own concerns. Hopefully, there would be more information, and trace evidence, when they returned to the crime scene.

CHAPTER FIVE

As they headed back to the Taylor home, Stella felt sure that the New Haven forensics team would have uncovered trace evidence by now to take them further.

With no obvious motives and no apparent reason for this bloody crime, the evidence in this case would be critical and she hoped it would guide their next steps.

When they approached the house, she saw one of the forensics team outside peeling off his gloves and footwear as he spoke to Grant.

"I hope you had a productive time," Stella said sympathetically. Working in such a bloodbath as Grant had described must have been nightmarish, even for a seasoned forensics expert.

The tall man turned to Stella looking as sickened as she'd expected. And more, too. Worryingly, he looked discouraged.

"Not so, ma'am," he said heavily.

"How do you mean?" Maxwell asked, sounding concerned.

"I mean that we have not picked up on any trace. It's unbelievable." He shook his head. "It's been years since I've come across a case that makes me doubt myself the way this one has, but that's how I feel right now. It seems impossible that this scene is so clean, but there's not a fingerprint. Not a hair. Only partial footprints and you can't tell their size or the sole pattern as there was an additional layer underneath."

Detective Grant looked as disturbed as Maxwell and Stella now felt.

"So what are we dealing with here?" he asked.

"It looks like a well-planned crime. The footprints show it. Whoever did this thought through every step. They didn't panic. They didn't make a mistake, and we sure could have used a mistake."

The forensic expert eased the head covering off, raked a hand through his gray hair, and wiped his forehead.

"This is not going to go down well with the media, and I've got a meeting with the local press just now. They're going to want answers," Grant said, sounding stressed.

"We're just going to have to keep digging and see what we can uncover," Stella said to Maxwell, but inside she felt unsure and helpless. It was as if the killer was already ten steps ahead of them, and gaining.

At that moment, another of the forensics team walked out of the house and began carefully peeling off his PPE while breathing deeply. Stella guessed the cold, fresh air tinged with the smell of the sea must be a relief after working the claustrophobic, blood-infused crime scene.

"This is surreal," he said to his tall colleague.

"I know. It's unbelievably clean of trace," the other man sympathized.

"Makes me want to go back in and check everything one more time. But we've already spent hours in there," he complained. "What are we going to find if we go back?"

"We can't find what isn't there."

"Nope," his colleague agreed.

"I was saying to the agents, it's been years since we've heard of a scene this clean," the other man observed.

Repeated, his words piqued Stella's interest.

"Years?" she asked the tall man, who was now gratefully hauling a cigarette out of his pack. "Have you worked a similar scene in the past?"

He gazed at her, his brown eyes narrowed thoughtfully. "Not personally, ma'am, but a colleague of mine who works in Delaware told us about a cold case at a conference we attended a while ago. I was thinking about it while I was working inside, because that one was also a double murder, a husband and wife. Also a scene that should have been a goldmine for trace, but there was none to be found. Thus, it went cold."

"It sounds identical," Maxwell said, looking motivated all over again.

"Not identical, because I do recall there was something taken from that home. An antique silver vase worth close to a million dollars was missing."

"How long ago was this?" Stella asked.

The forensics tech looked rueful. "Nine or ten years ago. Not a recent case, I'm afraid."

Even though the timeframe was long, Stella felt it was worth following up on. It could potentially be linked to other crimes in other states. Perhaps the killer moved around. Or perhaps it was a copycat crime.

"I wonder if anything was taken from this home," she said to Maxwell. "We should check that before we go any further."

"Can we go into the bedroom now?" Maxwell asked Grant.

"Sure. The work is finished, the bodies are removed, but it's still a mess. You're going to need foot covers and gloves for sure."

Feeling apprehensive about what she would find, but hopeful that there might be a clue to be discovered, Stella took another pair of foot covers out of the box, eased on a pair of gloves, and headed into the house. This time, she walked all the way down the corridor to the back of this large, sprawling home.

She smelled the blood when she was halfway along. It infiltrated her nostrils and prickled her spine, sending shivers of dread through her. It took her straight back to the moment she'd awakened, rising heavily out of a sleeping-pill-induced slumber to find Vaughn beside her, stabbed to death.

Her eyes narrowed as she saw the spatters of blood ahead. Behind her, she heard the hiss of Maxwell's breath as he took it in.

"We're dealing with a psycho here," he muttered, shaking his head vigorously as if trying to dislodge the terrible imaginings. "But it's not unheard of for a robber to torture his victims. It's unusual, but there is case history proving it."

Picking her way past the bloody pool, Stella went into the bedroom.

She immediately saw a pair of gold earrings on the bedside table. They were bright rose gold, in the shape of teardrops. Next to them, a gold bracelet lay half-hidden under a box of Kleenex.

"So it wasn't a robbery," Maxwell observed in a murmur, following the direction of her gaze.

"No, it can't have been the main reason," Stella agreed. "Unless there was one specific piece they were after."

Stella opened a drawer in the vanity and saw several more pieces of jewelry, together with a few pairs of expensive-looking sunglasses. Maxwell opened the cupboard on the husband's side of the bed. An iPad as well as a few hundred dollar bills were inside.

It looked as if robbery was not the main motive. But then Stella rethought.

"Perhaps the robbers only wanted what they had come for, and nothing else," she suggested. "The forensics tech mentioned that only one item was stolen in that other robbery, but it was a highly valuable item that would have fetched a big resale price in the right market. So maybe the same modus operandi applied here. Maybe only one item was stolen, and if so, it must have been something the killer knew about."

Maxwell narrowed his eyes thoughtfully.

"In that case, it might not even be in here. Something like a vase would surely have been on visible display. Nobody keeps an antique vase hidden away in their bedroom, do they? Shall we see if anything looks to be missing in the living room?"

Feeing relieved to be able to turn her back on this disturbing scene, Stella headed out of the bedroom.

CHAPTER SIX

Donny Davies couldn't believe his luck. Sometimes life was hard and times were tough. Other times, things aligned in a way that made him feel as if his bad luck was over and his big chance had arrived.

He knew that this time, he would need to be careful. He'd recently been paroled after serving a six-year sentence. No way did he want to go back. Not when he'd been dealt a potentially winning hand—if he played it right.

And he would need to play it right. He'd have to plan every step of the way to make the most of the windfall he deserved.

"I'm going to come across as an average guy who's broke and struggling, just looking to keep afloat and pay the school fees, seeing as how it's already the eighty-seventh of January," Donny decided, imagining the person he'd need to be to successfully make the sale without any alarm bells going off. Perhaps he could use that January joke when he was in the shop. It sounded witty and humble, like something an average guy would say when needing to sell something off while keeping his dignity.

He glanced at himself in the mirror, surprised again by how different his face looked after six years inside. Harder, thinner. It didn't look the same as the guy whose features had been on those Wanted posters back then.

It had been his own fault he'd been caught.

Sometimes, he couldn't help himself. Most times, he was the easiest going guy around, but other times, the anger just exploded out of him and he couldn't control it. He remembered those times well.

The cries of "Please don't hurt us!" inevitably brought out the violence in him. People shouldn't beg. Especially not when there was a weapon within easy reach. It had been their fault, not his, that he'd ended up getting so angry and hitting them just to keep them quiet.

In vivid color, the memory of his last few jobs came to mind. He'd promised to never go down that road. But somehow, he had.

The way the woman had screamed. "Don't! Please don't!"

He hadn't listened. Hadn't even heard her. All he'd wanted to do was silence her, as quickly and brutally as he could, because her whining and screaming and crying were distracting him from what he needed to do.

"You can't afford to be like that again," Donny told himself, feeling frustrated by the loss of control that could have ruined everything. Well, now those times were over. If he did things right, he'd never need to do another job like that.

He needed to control himself now, he thought, turning to stare at the shabby room where he'd spent the past two months of his life. It was a joyless place, cold and stark. But with any luck, he might never spend another night on that uncomfortable bed with its jutting springs.

In his hand, he held the bag that contained the treasure he needed and deserved, the item that was going to allow him to live a life of ease for the next while. No jobs to do. No anger. He would be able to chill out. To try and get past the static in his head that fizzed and sputtered so randomly, sparking him into decisions that shunted him further and further down a road he'd never really wanted to be on but now couldn't get back from.

But he had to do this right.

He juggled the bag from hand to hand, but gently, because although his reflexes were super-fast, he knew he needed to be careful with this item. What a find it had been! But he deserved it after what he'd handled in his life. He'd always known he was gifted. The man with the quick eyes and magic fingers. The person who could always come up with a story.

Searching through the meager clothes in his closet, he chose his best shirt. Threadbare and years old, it had originally been a quality item and looked the part. After some thought, Donny knotted a tie around his neck, letting out a disbelieving laugh because the last time he'd worn a tie had been when working as a bell-boy in his early twenties, before he'd stolen from a guest and been caught and lost his chances at working a normal nine to five.

Shoes—they needed to be shined. A guy walking in to sell this precious heirloom would shine his shoes. He'd be that kind of person. Respectable.

He rubbed a polish rag over them, and then slicked his hair back and squeezed a drop of gel, old and sticky, from the tube in his drawer. He wet his hands and gelled his unruly brown hair back. That was better. In line with the neat, conservative image he wanted to portray.

With the takings from this, he might even be able to buy a car. Start afresh.

Donny walked back to the mirror and smiled at himself. It wasn't a nice smile. Quickly, he adjusted it until it had that sad, guy-next-door quality. That was what he was aiming for. A harmless dude. Not someone who'd attack a screaming woman who was begging him not to hurt her. He wanted a poor, aw-shucks look.

He knew that some pawnbrokers didn't ask questions, but others did. So he needed to come across as legitimate, true-blue and genuine. A guy who'd inherited an item he had no use for and who was looking to sell it, because he, like everyone else, was experiencing tough times.

Donny himself was not sure of the item's value, though he knew from its intricacy and solid weight it was expensive. The gold had a hallmark. That, he knew about. But even so he'd need to assume he would be offered rock-bottom, a laughable amount.

He would then have to look shocked, and then pull himself together in a self-righteous way and go, "Sir, I appreciate you need to turn a profit. But I know that's too low. Please, make me a better offer on it, or I'll have to walk out and go somewhere else."

After that, it would be like a game of poker. Bluff and counterbluff until a deal was struck.

Donny felt filled with excitement at the thought of the riches to come. This could be the fresh start he needed. He could get out of state. He could contact that guy who said he would provide a fake ID that would stand up to any scrutiny. And he could hunker down somewhere warm, do a few odd jobs. No more police check-ins. A new life.

"Just control yourself," he told his reflection firmly. "And if they ask you where you got it, tell them it's a family heirloom."

He imagined the conversation that might play out.

"Where'd you get ahold of this, sir?"

Speaking in a quiet voice, making sure that smile looked humble and nice, he would explain, "It's my gran's." He corrected himself, wanting to sound more formal, like someone might do who would have inherited such an item. "Grandmother's. She recently passed."

"She did?" the other guy might then ask suspiciously.

"Grandma loved these pretty things. Her husband traveled a lot and was always picking up bargains and little treasures from antique stores. I remember this well, from the glass-fronted cupboard in her home. When she went into the retirement village, she packed everything up. She passed away in October, so when we got together over Christmas, we unpacked her boxes and shared them out. But I need to sell it. You know how it is. School fees, medical expenses. It's a fine piece, I'm sure, but we have no use for it as a family. What's the best deal you can do for me?" Then, adding a hint of worry into his voice, he could continue and say, "Or is it something I should sell through a specialist network? Do you think I'd get more for it there?"

Having set the bait, he hoped the dealer would walk straight into the trap and make him an immediate offer.

That was his story. It had to be his story.

He had to stay calm and give that dumb, good-natured grin that concealed the reality of what he could sometimes be.

Firmly suppressing the true facts about this heavy, gleaming, filigree object, Donny put the bag in his backpack and headed out of his room.

CHAPTER SEVEN

Stella stood in the hallway of the Taylor home, feeling preoccupied by the best and fastest way to find out if anything valuable was missing. A glance into the living room showed some shelves of ornaments. But how would they know if one piece was missing?

"We could get hold of their insurance company," she said to Maxwell. "They'll know what high value items they had stipulated in their policy. They can send us a checklist and we can compare that with the household contents."

"Yes. We definitely can do that. It will take time, though," Maxwell said. "And we won't know what they kept on display and what was locked away. They might have kept some valuables in a safe, or a safety deposit box. That could take even longer to source."

"But a random robber wouldn't know about anything locked away in a safe. Unless it was insider fraud. Someone corrupt, working for an insurance company and selling off the information," Stella said, revising her theory.

"That's also a possibility," Maxwell agreed.

She sighed, frustrated by the slowness of the options available to them. Her nerves still felt on edge after walking through the murder scene, with its grisly splashes of blood and faint metallic smell.

"If anything was stolen, it would have to be something that was in obvious view," she decided. "There were a few valuable-looking items in that home. A housekeeper would know exactly what was there. Do the Taylors have a housekeeper?"

Maxwell nodded. "They both work full time. In such a big home, they must surely have a housekeeper."

"Where is she and why was she not here this morning?"

Maxwell made a face. "She most probably arrived, saw the commotion, found out a few details, and decided to go home again. Not to say she was involved in the crime, but you know how it is. She might have been afraid, or not have wanted to show her face at such a time."

Stella nodded. “It’s going to take time to find her, then. We’ll need to look back through their phone records and they’ll only be available later. Unless someone in the neighborhood knows her.”

Her thoughts veered immediately to the helpful neighbor.

“Graham Haddow might know who she is.”

“Never mind that!” Looking excited, Maxwell turned to her. “Graham said he was in the home frequently for dinners. He might notice if anything is missing.”

“That’s true. Shall we ask him about the housekeeper, and also see if he could take a look? Just in the living room and dining room, perhaps? There’s nothing disturbing to see in those rooms. After all, he did say he’d be glad to help,” Stella said, hoping that he would keep his word, even if it meant setting foot in the home where this bloody double murder had occurred.

They headed across the road once more.

Stella tapped on the door, and Graham opened it, looking surprised.

“You’re back? What can I help with?” he asked.

“We came to ask you a favor,” she said.

“Sure. Whatever I can do, I will, as I said.” He nodded emphatically.

“We were wondering whether this case might be linked to a robbery. There was a similar case a long time ago where one very valuable item was taken from the home. We want to know if the same might have happened here.”

“And how can I help with that?” Graham now looked genuinely blank.

“Do you know if the Taylors had a housekeeper, and if they did, how we could contact her? She must know what was in the house, on the shelves, and could see if anything was missing.”

Graham looked back at her, his blue eyes narrowed in thought. He lifted a hand and rubbed it over his hair.

“I saw the housekeeper a few times. She’s a very cheerful woman. Maria is her name. Is she not at work this morning?”

“No. We think if she arrived, she would have been scared off and gone home.”

“Oh dear. I know she worked for them during the week and has done for years, but I unfortunately don’t have more information. I greeted her many times but never knew anything about her except her first name.”

"Thank you," Stella said, disappointed. They would be able to interview Maria and get her back to the house eventually. But that might be tomorrow, at the earliest.

Deciding to take a chance, she said, "Would you walk through the living room and dining room with us and take a look around? You said you were there regularly. You might notice if anything is missing."

Now, Graham looked conflicted.

"Go in there?" His voice held a note of panic. "I—I'm really not sure I can do that. After what happened inside? I don't think I would be up for it. No, no, no. This is not something I feel comfortable doing."

His hands were trembling again, Stella saw.

"We won't go anywhere near the crime scene," she tried, but he was shaking his head determinedly.

Sympathy and frustration collided inside her. Clearly, this was too far outside his comfort zone for him to even consider. There was nothing more she could do.

"That's fine. I understand."

Gritting her teeth over the delay, Stella turned away. As she walked back down the path, she fretted over what the next step should be. But, as she reached the road, she heard a shout behind her.

"Agent Fall! Agent Maxwell! Please, wait a moment!"

Surprised, Stella turned to see Graham hurrying stiffly behind them.

"Let me help you," he offered. "I had a knee-jerk reaction back there. I've rethought. More than anything else, I want this crime solved. And if walking into the house with you is what it takes, then I'll do it. I was familiar with their home and they often spoke about their art pieces and the stories behind them. I'm sure I would know if anything was gone. Please, let me come back in with you and at least take a look."

Stella felt hope rekindle as she met his direct blue gaze.

Graham had overcome his fears and that meant their investigation could speed up again.

"Thank you," she said gratefully.

They headed to the house, and Stella led the way back inside.

At the doorway, Graham hesitated a moment. He glanced over the road, toward the comfort and safety of his home. Then he turned back to the Taylor house, drew a deep breath, clasped his hands together, and stepped through the front door.

Thinking from Graham's perspective, she now realized what an intimidating thing it was to walk into the home.

“The living room is where they kept their collection of art and antiques,” Graham said. “Mark and Diane loved to travel, and Diane told me they always tried to pick up something special on their vacations.”

Stella noted that now he was speaking about the couple, his voice was growing more confident. Having overcome the psychological barrier of entering the house, she hoped he was starting to relax. That would mean he would think and observe more accurately.

Graham looked calm as he scanned the mantelpiece and the shelves.

“This is a Lladro ballerina,” he said, pointing to an exquisite porcelain dancer. The flowing lines of her dress were so detailed they looked like real fabric, only more beautiful, Stella thought.

“I remember they bought that ballerina while in Spain. And these two glass paperweights they picked up in France. Murano glass, I believe, and quite valuable. Very beautiful, don’t you think, with their floral interiors?” Graham glanced sadly at Stella, before looking back at the flawless glass globes with the explosions of color within.

“They are beautiful,” Stella agreed.

Graham walked slowly around the room, looking puzzled.

“I can’t see anything that should be here and isn’t.” He scanned the shelves, shaking his head.

Stella looked at Maxwell, her expression clearly conveying his own thoughts: Oh well. We tried.

She began running through the next options in her mind, deciding which should be done first. The insurance company might be a quicker option than the housekeeper, but not if the New Haven offices could unlock the Taylor’s phones fast enough. If they could, the housekeeper might be the better choice.

But then Graham drew in his breath with a shocked gasp.

“Wait! I’ve realized what’s missing!”

As one, Stella and Maxwell spun around to face him. Excitement prickled Stella’s skin. Something had been taken!

“It’s the Fabergé egg. It’s extremely valuable. I remember Diane explained it’s not one of the originals, but it’s a replica made in the early 1900s. They didn’t just buy it. You couldn’t just buy an item like that today, it’s too rare. They inherited it from Diane’s great-aunt. Or maybe it was Mark’s great-aunt. I don’t remember now.”

In his enthusiasm, Graham was rambling on, but Stella felt unbelievably grateful to him. Thanks to this observation, they could now take the next step.

“Can you describe the egg?” Stella asked.

“It was about so high.” Graham held his hands a short distance apart. “Egg shaped, of course, and crafted from gold with ruby red insets. It stood on fine, scroll legs, also made from gold. I believe the egg was solid gold, and contained a number of diamonds and rubies. If I recall, they were not planning to keep it. They didn’t have children and I know Diane felt it needed to be passed on. I believe they were going to gift it to Mark’s eldest nephew for his twenty-first birthday next year.”

“I can’t tell you how much we appreciate this help. I know it wasn’t easy for you. But it’s given us a great lead. We have to go to the New Haven police department now and make some calls.” Stella felt as if this investigation had just veered into the fast lane. Now, they had evidence to chase.

“Please let me know how it turns out,” Graham said, sounding as hopeful as Stella felt.

As soon as they had seen him safely across the road, Stella and Maxwell rushed for the car.

“Don’t even wait till we get there,” Maxwell said. “Let’s call ahead and get started right now.”

Quickly, Stella dialed Grant, who picked up within the first ring.

“We’ve discovered that a valuable Fabergé egg is missing from the home,” Stella said. “It’s likely that the thief wouldn’t want to hold onto this and would want to get it sold before anyone realized it was missing. So we need help. We urgently have to contact all the local places—the secondhand dealers, the pawnbrokers, even the jewelers in the area. We need to track this down and get an ID on the person who sold it.”

“I’m on it,” Grant said. “Send me a description of the item and I’ll get my team working on that right away.”

Keying in the description Graham had given her, Stella felt confident that the case was gaining momentum. Finding out where this item had been sold would provide a strong lead to the killer. Now it was a race against time. They needed to track down the Fabergé egg before the robber fled the state.

CHAPTER EIGHT

Walking into the New Haven police department's back room, which was noisy with the trilling of phones and the thrum of printers, Stella saw two constables were already gathering information on the area's secondhand stores.

"Good morning, Agents." The female constable looked up from the pages spread over the desk, her face flushed with excitement under her curly brown hairstyle. "We've checked the city database for anything resembling the egg but nothing has been entered so far. We've compiled a list of all the pawnbrokers and secondhand stores within a ten-mile radius of the Taylors' home address. We're now going to start on the jewelry stores, but we both thought that a pawnbroker would be the first choice for this kind of sale. I hope that's right?"

"That's great. Good thinking," Stella praised her.

"Let's get started with the calls," Maxwell said.

The back room was a hive of activity, with groups of police working in several different cubicles on various cases. There was only one spare desk in the room, so after picking up the printed list, she and Maxwell hustled over to it and got busy on the phone.

"I'll take the first number, you take the next, and we alternate?" she suggested.

Maxwell nodded, and Stella scooted over to the far side of the desk, punching in the number for Main Street Cash Sales.

It rang twice before it was picked up by a throaty-voiced man who sounded as if he might have a sixty-a-day habit.

"FBI Agent Fall on the line," Stella said. "We're tracing a stolen item. We need to know if you received anything for sale this morning."

There was a surprised silence on the other end.

"Sure. I have had a couple of things in this morning that haven't yet been entered into the system. What item is that?"

"It's an egg-shaped ornament. The full description is a Fabergé egg. It's a gold and red item, probably about the size of your hand."

"No, ma'am." The store attendant sounded relieved to be able to give a negative answer. "Nothing like that's come in today."

“Thank you,” Stella said, turning to the third one on the list, just as Maxwell took the fourth.

“FBI Agent Fall on the line,” she said again when the call was picked up. “We’re tracing a stolen item and—”

“What would that be?” the man interrupted her.

He sounded sharp and wary. Stella wondered if that wariness was because he had, in fact, recently acquired a very valuable new item.

“It’s a Fabergé egg. Gold and red. It would have been brought in this morning,” Stella abbreviated her description.

The man sighed.

“Yes. I did have someone bring in the item about half an hour ago. I was sure it was a genuine sale, though,” he added hurriedly. “I’m surprised to hear it was stolen. I was going to enter it on the database as soon as I could, of course.”

Even though Stella personally doubted his good intentions, triumph flared inside her. They had results, and faster than she’d hoped, thanks to the quick work from the New Haven team. She felt as if this shadowy killer was now no longer anonymous but real and exposed.

Quickly, Stella checked the address on record for the store.

“You’re at 17 Greengage Street in New Haven?”

“That’s correct.”

“We’re on our way. Please make sure that we can access your security camera footage when we get there,” Stella said.

Maxwell had picked up on her conversation and quickly ended his own call. She saw her excitement mirrored in his eyes as she stood up, grabbing her purse.

“Greengage Street it is,” Maxwell said. “Let’s go see what our robber looks like.”

They headed out of the police station and ran to where the car was parked. Climbing inside, Stella knew that every second counted now. With the sale made, the robber would want to leave town as soon as he could.

Anxiety knotted inside her as they sped along the main road. She reassured herself by remembering that at least this pawn shop was close to the police department. In fact, she could see Greengage Street ahead already.

The street was strategically located in the no-man’s-land between respectable suburbs and a more run-down part of town. They parked outside the shop, which had a large, faded signboard above the door. In the windows, Stella saw a wide variety of goods for sale. Anything from leather jackets to scooters to kitchen appliances could be purchased here.

Walking in, she breathed in the musty smell she'd expected that was associated with shops where secondhand items sometimes stood for long periods of time.

Behind the counter was a forty-something-year-old man with eyes that looked a decade older than his actual age. Stella guessed that you got to see way more than your share of human desperation working in a place like this. As they walked in, he was handing cash to a stressed-looking woman in exchange for a smart, shiny mountain bike. The woman turned and left quickly, without making any eye contact with Stella or Maxwell.

The man wheeled the bike to the back of the shop and then returned, checking them out through those world-weary eyes.

"You'll be the FBI, right?" he asked.

Maxwell nodded. "Your name?" he asked.

"Paulo Diego."

"You the owner?"

"Yes. I'm the owner. What's the story with this item?" he asked.

"It went missing from the home after a husband and wife were murdered last night," Stella said.

Paulo's eyebrows shot up in surprise.

"No way," he said.

"Why do you say that?" Maxwell asked.

"The guy who brought it in was just a normal customer, I'd swear to it. Typical working-class man, down on his luck and embarrassed about needing to sell off part of his inheritance."

"You think? Or just a good actor?" Maxwell didn't sound convinced.

Paulo shrugged defensively. "I guess he could have been, but he didn't come across that way. In any case, I'll fetch it for you. And you can see the footage, and the guy's name and address details. For what they're worth," he said, sounding more doubtful now about these credentials.

He disappeared through the back door and Stella guessed he was opening a safe. She was sure he'd stashed it in there even before the FBI had called. He must have estimated the item's high value immediately.

He brought it back. Stella stared at it with interest.

It certainly was a beautiful egg. The gold gleamed richly in the store's dusty light and tiny diamonds sparkled. The intricately woven red detail was brighter and more vivid than she'd imagined. The stand itself was incredibly dainty; the perfect foil for the solid egg.

"It opens up. Inside there's a rose," Paulo explained. "The gold is real; it's hallmarked. I'm guessing the stones are real. The diamonds passed my basic testing."

"How much did you pay him?" she asked.

"Twenty thousand dollars."

"You got a good deal there." Given the quality of the materials, Stella was sure this item must be worth at least half a million.

"He was happy, too," Paulo said defensively.

Had he been, receiving twenty thousand dollars for a quick sale to a pawnbroker?

Something was feeling strange. Would it have been worth preplanning, breaking in, and committing the most serious of crimes, for the robber to end up being shortchanged on the item's sale? It was puzzling. Perhaps he'd realized the trouble he would be in and had decided to cut his losses and flee. Perhaps another buyer had been lined up and fallen through.

Criminals' motives didn't always make sense, she knew, and the best way to find out would be to find him.

"Can we see your footage. And his ID?" Stella cut to the chase.

"Sure. It's all in the back office."

"Let's go in there and take a look," she said.

Now that they had confirmation of the deal, the chase was on was to find the man who had sold this valuable ornament.

"Here's the copy of his ID," Paulo said.

"Donald Davies?" The date of birth showed him to be thirty-three, Stella saw. He'd also provided an address and a phone number. Stella guessed those were more than likely fake.

"He said his name was Donny," the pawnbroker agreed.

The photo was small and blurred and looked to be a few years old. Stella couldn't get any impression of his features from this flat, black-and-white photocopy. She also barely pick up the address. It was a driver's license, old and worn. It looked legitimate enough, but the address, assuming she was reading the blurry letters and numbers correctly, would in any case be years old and probably out of date.

"I'll get the camera footage now," Paulo said.

"How tall was he?" Stella asked, as Paulo turned to his computer with a frown of concentration.

"About my height. So that would be five-ten."

"Weight?"

"He was a slim guy. Skinny. Not fat; not well built. Here's the footage."

The focus in the room sharpened as Stella and Maxwell stared at the replay of this important meeting.

The man who walked in did look the part, Stella saw. She actually couldn't blame the pawnbroker for having bought the story. He wore a shirt with a collar and tie, and dark pants. His brown hair was neatly slicked back. He exuded slightly desperate respectability.

Donald Davies was a good actor, Stella decided.

"Pause it there," she asked. That moment gave them a good view of his profile. High forehead, sharp nose, weak chin.

Concentrating hard and taking in every moment of the footage, Stella now had a good impression of the basic looks, height, and demeanor of this man, as well as his name and his exact age.

"Please send through this footage now, and the copy of the ID," she said, writing her email down for him.

"The New Haven police will be here soon to seize the item, so make sure it goes back in the safe," Maxwell said.

Paolo's eyes widened at the thought of the lost money.

"It's stolen goods. If we find Mr. Davies and he has the cash on him, we will refund you." From the tone of Maxwell's voice, Stella could hear he didn't think the chances were good.

But what were their chances of finding him?

Panic seized her as she thought about how far away he could already be. But no, she told herself. Once the deal was done and he had the cash in his hand, there would be no reason for Donny to have fled in a panic. He would at least have to pack his things.

They hustled out of the shop, climbed into the car, and made the calls right there in the parking lot outside the pawn shop.

Maxwell tried the phone number, which proved to be the waste of time Stella thought it would be. The number didn't exist. Then he keyed the address into his map.

The address didn't exist either. Surprisingly, there wasn't a 1001 Wallflower Avenue in New Haven.

"So near but yet so far," Maxwell said, tension thrumming in his voice.

An idea occurred to Stella.

"Do you think he might have a record? A guy like that, committing robberies, could have been inside in the past. If he was, the parole officers might have his real address."

Maxwell got on the line to New Haven and asked to speak directly to Grant.

"Donald Davies. We're battling to trace him and thought he might have a record. If so, could you get address details for him?"

"I'll check with the parole department. Give me a few minutes and I'll call you back. If he is a paroled prisoner, he's likely to be living west of downtown, between the prison and the police station. That's where most paroled inmates go, if you want to start driving in that direction," Grant advised.

Maxwell accelerated through the streets of New Haven. It was now lunch time, and traffic was heavier. Around her, Stella felt a sense of unreality that life was happening as normal. People were heading out from the office to grab some food, or climbing into the car to fetch the kids from school. And she and Maxwell were racing across town in pursuit of a violent criminal.

At that moment, Maxwell's phone rang. He grabbed it up.

"Donald Davies does have a record. He's been inside twice for violent robbery and assault," Grant said. "He was paroled two months ago. When I called, they said he missed a check-in this morning."

Stella clenched her fists in triumph.

"What's his recorded address?"

"Summertown Heights, building three, apartment 401."

Maxwell nodded. "That's in the direction we're headed. But it's likely he'll try to skip town, especially if he's missed a parole check-in. We need to urgently organize roadblocks on all the major routes out and search all vehicles."

"I'll get the police onto it."

With a parole check-in skipped, Stella knew they were now under severe pressure of time. Roadblocks would take a while to organize. It could be too late by the time they were in place.

As Grant disconnected the call, Stella and Maxwell pulled up outside Summertown Heights. The name was the prettiest part of this dilapidated-looking housing tract, set among cracked paving and raw concrete surrounds. Outside the building was a shriveled tree that looked to be dead. The only other greenery was provided by a few tall weeds pushing through the gaps.

"Building 3. There it is."

Stella didn't trust the elevator in a place like this and Maxwell was clearly on the same page. They rushed toward the stairs, and taking them two at a time, headed up to the fourth floor.

Stella decided to chance going left, and it paid off. She passed 405, then 404, and breaking into a run, sprinted to the apartment all the way at the end.

The door was closed. Stella grabbed the handle.

To her surprise, it opened instantly.

They stared into an empty room that looked to have been hastily abandoned. The covers on the single bed, which looked dirty, were still creased. The wardrobe doors hung open revealing empty shelves inside. Only a couple of crumpled items of clothing remained.

"He's gone," Maxwell said flatly.

"He ran. He's not coming back," Stella agreed, feeling devastated as she stared at the evidence. They must have just missed him. If they'd only been a half hour earlier they might have caught him as he ran around the room, grabbing his possessions, getting ready to flee.

A thought occurred to Stella.

"Does he own a car? He might not if he's been in jail for years. Let's think through the logistics of how he did this."

Maxwell grabbed his phone and a moment later, he was connected up with Grant again.

"Question," he said. "Does the suspect have a vehicle registered in his name?"

"Let me check," Grant said.

Maxwell held on, tapping his feet impatiently as he accessed the records.

"No. No vehicle," Grant confirmed. "We've given a visual description to the police who are setting up the roadblocks."

"Thanks," Maxwell said.

"I don't think he's driving out of here," Stella said. "I think he's going to flee some other way. He doesn't have a car. I doubt he has a friend who's willing to take a long drive with a person who's basically a fugitive. He has his belongings with him so hitching a ride would be difficult. It would expose him, and also, he'd have no guarantee of when or where he would get a ride."

"That leaves bus or train."

"Train is quicker. And also, this apartment complex is close to the station." Pacing across the dusty floor, Stella peered out of the small window, its glass streaked with grime. "You can actually see the train tracks from here. Take a look. That would influence his decision if he was leaving in a hurry with a big bag. He'd think about the trains, because he sees and hears them all day. My feeling is he packed his gear, and he headed out on foot to the station."

Maxwell joined her at the window, glancing from the unappealing view down to the map on his phone.

"Let's go to the station now. If we've guessed right, we might be able to catch up with him before he gets on the train."

They rushed back down the stairs, going so fast that Stella reckoned they got down to street level faster than the elevator could possibly have done. They raced to the car and jumped in. Then Maxwell set off, swerving to avoid a pothole and swerving again to miss a bottle lying in the road.

This was a tough part of town. The wrong side of the tracks, for sure. But the tracks might lead them to the fleeing perpetrator of this violent crime.

CHAPTER NINE

Stella ran into the New Haven Union Station's historic building feeling breathless with tension. So much was riding on her hunch that Donny had fled by train. This was make or break. What happened in the next few minutes could affect the entire outcome of this case.

Inside the high-roofed interior, she slowed for a moment, taking stock of her surroundings, hoping that by a miracle she might see Donny immediately.

The station was bigger and busier than she'd expected. Donny's apartment complex might have been on the wrong side of the tracks, but this enormous and stately building was all the way on the right side. Ranks of polished wooden benches were positioned down the center of the large building. Here, commuters were sitting and waiting for trains. The wintry light glowed through arched windows set high in the walls, and large round lamps hung from the ceiling, which featured a mosaic of intricately patterned squares.

The station itself looked neat, clean, and organized, with a multitude of travelers walking purposefully to and from the platforms.

Where in the crowds could she find one man who had already proven to be an expert in disguising himself to play the part? Was he still wearing the shirt and tie he'd used when visiting the pawnbroker? Stella suspected he might have changed his clothes.

Where would he be heading? Did he have a plan or was he just looking to take the fastest, farthest train he could out of here? How could they locate him?

There were lines of people at the ticket sales kiosks and the self-service booths. There were clusters around the fast food shop fronts. Surely he would not have stopped for food at such a pressured time?

Side by side, she and Maxwell paced through the main station, hoping to spot this man who unfortunately was average looking in every way. With January's chill in the air, people were wrapped in coats and hats, scarves and jackets, making the challenge even more difficult.

Stella felt a flash of cold panic as she wondered if they'd guessed completely wrong. Perhaps he hadn't taken the train at all. He could be somewhere else entirely. He could have stowed away in a long distance truck and be cruising past the roadblocks even as they searched here.

Have faith in yourself. She knew that's what Clem, the retired FBI agent who had been her university mentor, would say. Clem would tell her that she'd arrived here as a result of a deductive process which was based partly on intuition and partly on the information she'd picked up—both obvious and subliminal signs.

Now that she was here, she needed to take that process all the way and stop doubting herself. The train tracks had been there, right outside his window. The tracks would have been the first place his thoughts went when he decided to flee.

"We should check the platforms in order of the departure times," Maxwell decided. "It looks like the first train is going to Washington, D.C. That's on platform two, in five minutes."

"Good plan," Stella agreed.

D.C. was far enough away to appeal to a robber on the run, Stella thought. It would provide a hub from where he could head down south, seeking a warmer city to hunker down, hide out, and live off his ill-gotten gains.

They turned and rushed toward the platforms, threading their way through slower-moving passengers, with Stella intently scanning the faces of each one as they turned to her in annoyance.

But Donald would be keeping his face hidden. Stella was sure that this experienced criminal would know all the tricks for keeping low. If he was jostled or bumped, he would just look down.

How could they find him among so many? she wondered, as she walked toward the closest platform. This suddenly seemed like an impossible task. He was good at blending in, becoming average and unnoticeable. They'd seen it in the video.

Arriving at the platform, Stella saw that every departing passenger had their back to them. They were looking at the train, waiting for the doors to open. It was impossible to see who was who, and they didn't have time to fight their way through the tightly pressed group of commuters.

"Damn," Maxwell muttered, slowing as they reached the edge of the crowd. "There's no way we can see him here."

Unless… The spark of an idea came to her. Would her wild plan work? They had only moments to try before the doors opened and the passengers flowed on and off the train.

"I'm going to call out to him," she warned Maxwell.

Just in time, Stella remembered that this violent robber went by a harmless-sounding nickname rather than his full name.

As the doors hissed open and the passengers began pushing forward, she yelled out at the top of her voice, "Hey, Donny! Donny! Wait up!"

A few of the passengers closest to her glanced around in annoyance at the decibel levels, but Stella didn't even notice them. As she yelled, she was scanning the crowd for that involuntary response, the automatic head-turn that somebody would give on hearing their name.

And she saw it.

At the far end of the platform, a man with a scarf swathed around his neck and a baseball cap on his head looked around, briefly and automatically. The glance at his profile told Stella all she needed to know.

"That's him!"

At that moment, Donny's appalled gaze met hers.

He turned and began running along the platform, away from them.

"Stop!" Stella yelled, pushing through the crowds in pursuit. Adrenaline surged inside her as she and Maxwell raced along the platform, their shoes thudding on the concrete. He wasn't going to board the train. He had abandoned that idea. So where would he go?

To her shock, when he was past the length of the train, Donny answered that question in a way she'd never expected. He jumped down onto the tracks themselves.

Racing ahead of her, Maxwell didn't hesitate. He launched himself off the platform, skidding onto the gravel below. Stella heard the warning blare of the train's horn as Maxwell's shoes slipped on the slick metal and scrunched over the coarse stones.

Breathing hard, Stella stopped and thought.

Where was Donny going? There was nowhere for him to go but up the other side, and back out of the station. Maxwell was fast and agile, but Donny had the speed of desperation, and could be aiming to double back and lose him in the station's crowds.

She could follow, but she was slower than both the men would be. Or she could also double back, anticipating that Donny would return to the station.

Deciding on the more strategic move, Stella turned around and sprinted back the way she had come, hoping that she'd made the best call in the split-second circumstances. A two-pronged approach would be better than one, even though she was now getting caught up in the crowds. Some people were standing still, watching with interest as the chase played out. But others, who hadn't noticed the drama, were going about their day, wheeling their bags, talking on their phones.

A man veered to the side ahead of her in the throes of a conversation. She almost collided with him, twisting to the left, hearing his annoyed shout behind her and the thump as he dropped his briefcase.

There wasn't a moment to apologize or help him. There wasn't time for anything except chasing down this robber who was now on the run. She imagined Maxwell, pursuing him along the tracks. At some stage Donny would have to jump up onto another platform. He would have to reenter the station.

Scenarios unfolded in her mind as she pounded into the station itself.

Gasping for breath, Stella slowed and looked around. She couldn't see either Donny or Maxwell. Perhaps they had run all the way to the last platform before heading out?

But, as she prepared to race there, Stella stopped herself.

Donny was cunning and desperate. He'd shown himself to be good at thinking on his feet.

His mad dash onto the tracks had been a distraction. He'd wanted to lure them away, make them believe he was running to the exit.

But perhaps Donny had never meant to do that at all. What if he'd tried to lead them away and lose them for a moment, so that he could double back and go where he'd been planning all along?

That was to board the train. Donny had a ticket, he wanted to skip the state, and he wasn't going to let the FBI stop him.

Wishing she'd understood his strategy earlier, Stella hurtled back through the station and veered in the direction of platform two.

The passengers had mostly boarded the train. Stella cast her mind back to that baseball cap. A faded taupe. Not distinctive. But she could remember how it looked.

Outside a whistle blew loudly. An announcement boomed. The train was about to leave.

Stella agonized for one indecisive moment. Was this hunch right? Maxwell was nowhere to be seen and the train was on the point of leaving.

But if it left and he'd managed to sneak back inside, then he'd be gone.

She darted into the train, knowing she had only a minute before those doors whooshed closed and it departed. She raced down the corridor, jostling against people who were still getting into their seats. Glancing from left to right, she hoped desperately for a sign of that faded cap, or Donny's badly gelled hair.

Nothing here. Perhaps he was in the next carriage. She couldn't give up now. She had to keep looking. She rushed along the ranks of seats, knowing time was running out, anxiety flaring inside her.

Perhaps she should try calling again, she thought. And this time, if she yelled really loud, she could keep a lookout for the only guy who didn't look around.

"Donny!" she yelled. Sure enough, practically every person in the carriage glanced back.

And then, ahead of her, she saw him. Hunched down in the seat, looking totally inconspicuous. His head was bowed. Only that faded cap gave his presence away.

Stella ran to him, pushing past an annoyed-looking woman with a gabbled apology.

He looked up as she arrived, looking horrified. She grabbed his arm, hoping that he would come with her willingly and wouldn't start fighting, because she couldn't pull her gun on a crowded train. There was far too much risk something would go wrong.

"FBI," she said breathlessly. "Donald Davies, you are under arrest."

"No!" he shouted, panic in his tone. "I've done nothing wrong! Leave me alone!"

She grabbed his arm, and as she did so, his face changed. The innocent expression vanished. Raw fury blazed from his eyes. He tried to pull away from her, twisting his arm viciously out of her grasp so that she had to cling onto the rough fabric of his coat. He struggled to his feet, trying to shove her aside with his other arm.

"Hey! Stop that!" someone shouted, but nobody tried to help. Instead, the nearby passengers scattered. She was in this on her own, with a struggling man who was stronger than he looked, and a train that was on the point of departing.

"Come with me!" Latching onto his arm again, Stella did her best to twist it up behind him. He kicked out viciously, missing her shin by a hair's breadth. Stella dragged him backward, her heart hammering as the whistle shrilled again.

"You're under arrest," she shouted again, breathlessly, jerking his arm so that he staggered back, but he clung desperately to the seat and she couldn't budge him.

And then, with footsteps pounding, Maxwell jumped onto the train.

He raced to where she was struggling with her uncooperative captor and grabbed his other arm.

"Get off this train, now," he snapped at Donny.

The whistle screamed again, a final time. Stella took hold of his wrist and tugged the stringy, struggling man down the corridor toward the door, with Maxwell shoving him from behind.

They reached the doorway just as the doors hissed shut. Stella stuck her arm out and forced them back, leaping out of the train and pulling Donny with her as Maxwell jumped out behind.

In the struggle, Donny cartwheeled to the ground and Stella thumped painfully down on her knees, hanging onto his wrists with all her might as Maxwell wrestled the cuffs onto him. With a clicking and a whooshing, the train pulled smoothly away.

At the very last second, they'd managed to apprehend their suspect.

Bruised, battered, and feeling stunned that they'd won this race against the clock, Stella scrambled to her feet.

It was time to question Donald Davies, and get the truth about his involvement in this double murder.

CHAPTER TEN

After the chilly draftiness of the station platform, Stella felt relieved to walk into the warm interview room at the New Haven police precinct. She felt even more relieved that their prime suspect was seated at the table. His baseball cap had been removed to reveal a mop of unruly hair that still had traces of gel in it. His hands were cuffed behind him.

"I didn't do it," he gabbled, as soon as Stella and Maxwell entered the room.

"Didn't do what?" Maxwell asked cynically.

Stella took a seat opposite the guilty-looking man. Maxwell stood with his arms folded, glaring intimidatingly down at him.

"I didn't steal it. I know why you've brought me in. It was because of that golden egg. I'm not stupid. I know the pawn shop guy probably alerted you."

He'd still had most of the cash on him when he was arrested. For sure, he'd been planning on a quick run and a fresh start elsewhere. Stella knew the pawnbroker would be surprised to get the money back.

"He didn't alert us. We tracked you down ourselves. Where did you obtain this item?"

"I found it."

"Found it where? On a shelf in the owner's home?" Maxwell asked.

"No!" Donny shook his head and Stella saw a trace of his former aggression in the jut of his chin. "Don't make me out to be a liar when I'm telling you the truth!"

"The truth?" Maxwell's voice rose incredulously. "You told the pawnbroker you'd inherited it from your grandma. You have a criminal record of violent robberies. You've recently come out of prison. You said you were innocent when you missed a parole check-in today. Parole violation is a crime. You're not innocent. The only question is what you're guilty of." Maxwell glared at him.

"I swear, I found it. It was by the side of the road, near a street corner downtown. I can show you exactly where."

"And it was just lying there?" Maxwell asked.

Donny nodded. "It was under a bush, wrapped in a clear plastic packet. I first thought someone had thrown it out of a car but then I thought that would have damaged it. So then I thought someone must have dropped it. Like, it fell out of a bag or a pocket."

Watching this exchange, Stella could see Maxwell was more and more convinced that Donny was lying about everything. But she wasn't as sold on the concept anymore. With a flash of worry, Stella remembered all the other treasures that had been untouched and undamaged in the house.

She remembered her earlier thought that a specialist robber, entering a home to acquire just one object of high value, would have had a good idea of that object's value and would probably also have had an established network through which to sell it. He wouldn't have arrived hopefully at the nearest pawnbroker with a hard-luck story, and accepted a payment that was ludicrously below its value.

If he had stolen the item with the intention of pawning it, why not pick up another few things as well? Gold, for example. Gold jewelry was far easier to sell quickly than this unique ornament, and often with fewer questions asked.

In a true robbery, other valuables should have disappeared for good. Melted into thin air, never to have been seen again.

"Where were you last night?" she asked Donny, and watched his eyes narrow.

That wasn't a question he wanted to answer.

"I wasn't stealing that trinket," Donny muttered, sounding defiant. "I've got rights. I don't have to tell you where I was. You picked me up for all the wrong reasons. Let's get in the car now, and I will show you where I found that item."

"Show me on the map," Maxwell said.

They hadn't yet told him in what area the crime had taken place. That was a trap he would have to avoid.

Maxwell opened up a paper map of downtown New Haven. Donny peered down, his eyes narrowed as he made out the maze of streets.

With a finger, he pointed.

The corner that Donny indicated was three miles away from the scene of the crime. It was a very different part of New Haven, though. A lower income area, with denser housing.

But it was in the vicinity of the crime. That was for sure. Donny had now admitted he'd been within three miles of the murder scene.

Perhaps she had been wrong, Stella thought. He could have been working with an accomplice and picked up the item from a prearranged place. Or he could simply be lying. Lies didn't have to make sense. When people were desperate, they often didn't.

"What were you doing in that part of New Haven?" Stella asked him.

"I was—I was visiting a friend. That's all. Just visiting a friend."

"I don't believe you," Stella said. "What friend do you have in that area?"

"I can't give the name," Donny insisted.

"You say you picked the item up this morning? Then where were you last night?" Maxwell asked again. "Between the hours of eight p.m. and—let's say—midnight? Are your movements accounted for? Perhaps there's someone who can confirm them? Because, if you do not have an alibi, we're going to keep you detained on suspicion of the crime. And you'll be detained a long, long time," he added threateningly.

Donny was going pale.

"What—what crime is this?"

"You should know. You were there," Maxwell told him in a hard voice.

"Where?" Now there was panic in the other man's tone. "What are you implying I did?"

"We know you commit violent robberies. Your record proves it. And this was a violent robbery, only you didn't stop at assaulting the homeowners. You murdered them!"

Maxwell stepped menacingly toward the other man.

"No!" Donny cried out in shock. Fear had leached all the color from his face. "I didn't do such a thing! I wouldn't ever kill someone. I mean I—I know I've been—a bit rough in the past, on a job. I tell people to be quiet, they need to be quiet for their own safety. But murder? You got the wrong guy!" he pleaded.

"Then tell us where you were," Maxwell insisted.

Donny bit his lip, his yellowed teeth stabbing into the flesh so hard Stella thought he might draw blood. He was clearly overstressed by the question. She had no idea what had triggered this extreme response.

"I can't," he muttered.

"That's fine. Then we keep you inside until you're ready to tell us. We'll start listing the charges in the meantime." Maxwell stared stonily at him.

"Please, no." Donny shook his head violently.

"Whatever it is, it surely can't be worse than murder? So if you do have an alibi, you need to disclose it," Stella pushed him.

There must be a compelling reason why Donny did not want to reveal his whereabouts on the night of the crime. And there was only one reason it could be, Stella realized, with a flash of insight.

"You were on another job, weren't you?" she asked, and watched his shoulders slump in defeat.

"I was breaking into a house," he admitted.

Stella nodded. "It's okay. Tell us. Whatever happened there, it won't be as bad as what you'll be up against if we can't confirm your alibi."

Reluctantly, Donny spilled the beans. "Number eighteen Dauphine Avenue. I'd—I'd been past there last week on trash collection day. I saw they'd purchased a new TV. I was outside from about nine p.m. until eleven. At eleven I broke in downstairs. I got the TV as well as a few other things. But then the homeowners woke up. I heard them shouting upstairs so I fled. I didn't hurt anyone, I swear. I don't do that anymore. I managed to get the TV out and hid in a park. I called my contact who's a fence. He came through at about two and collected the things and paid me out. So—so that is where I was last night. I was doing another job."

"And this morning?"

"It was trash collection day again. I was scoping out the area, looking for any other boxes and packages," Donny admitted miserably. "That was when I saw this thing lying there."

Stella's hopes crashed down around her and she saw the hardness of disappointment in Maxwell's eyes.

"We're going to check that out," he said sharply. He and Stella stood and walked out of the interview room.

"I can't believe it," Maxwell muttered as soon as the door was closed. "But at the same time, I can. This whole situation is so weird. Why would someone take that Fabergé egg out of the home and then just dump it by the roadside?"

"I can believe it, too. This wasn't a robbery," Stella whispered back. "It was set up to look like one, but it's almost as if they didn't care if the item was found."

"That other murder where the vase was stolen can't be related to this one then."

Stella nodded. "It's far less likely now that we know this egg was just dumped." She sighed. "I feel we've been played. Not by him, but by whoever really did this. I feel like the killer is taunting us. Perhaps we need to go back and look at who knew the Taylors well. There must be a personal connection to the killing. We need to start looking in more detail at their contacts. Their friends. And find out who was angry enough with them to set up such a thing."

CHAPTER ELEVEN

As Stella headed to the police precinct's back office, her phone rang. Checking the caller ID, she saw it was Viv.

"I need to take this. It could be urgent," she said to Maxwell, walking quickly away from him down a corridor that led to the precinct's utility and storage rooms.

Why was Viv calling? Stella hoped she wasn't in any trouble. Her refusal to go into a safe house worried Stella deeply.

"Viv!" As soon as she was far enough away to be out of earshot, Stella answered.

"Stella." Satisfaction radiated from Viv's voice. "I'm leaving the bank. That evidence I told you about? I just collected some of it from the safe deposit box where I've kept it. Things are moving forward. My meeting is first thing in the morning. By this time tomorrow, we will have him. He won't be able to come back from this."

"Are you going straight home?" Stella asked.

"No. I've got two more stops. I'll be home in a few more hours and I will make sure the place is locked up tight."

Stella bit her lip. "Tonight, you really should go somewhere else."

"I'll be fine!" Viv protested.

Stella decided she was not going to take this for an answer. Drawing on all her persuasive powers, she spoke calmly but with as much force as she could manage.

"It's just for one night. It could be the most important night of your life. You don't want anything to go wrong. You don't want anyone to break in and steal your evidence. I am imploring you. Please, get out of town for tonight. Make a last-minute booking somewhere in a different name. Leave your car behind. Take the train or take a cab. Please. Just for me, will you do this?"

Viv sighed. "Okay, Stella," she said. "Just for you, I will sleep somewhere else. I have an idea where I can go. It's a private place where I know they won't find me. And I will take a cab and leave my car at home. I'll have to go back this afternoon to pack, but I won't stay home."

Stella felt the tension inside her unwind just a little.

“It will be the safest option, for sure. Thank you for doing it.”

“I can’t wait until things are normal again and I don’t have to watch my back like this,” Viv said in a heartfelt tone.

“Be safe,” Stella said before ending the call.

Feeling thankful that Viv had agreed to hide away for this critical time, Stella walked through to the police station’s back office, where Maxwell was seated at a desk.

“Good news,” he said. “Diane Taylor’s phone has been unlocked. The tech said he’s on his way here with it. While we wait, I’ve got another lead—one of Mark’s closest friends who saw him regularly. His name is Richard. He called the New Haven police department after he heard what had happened, looking for more information on the death. I spoke to him, and he said he’d meet me here to tell me what he knew about the two of them.”

“That could be very useful,” Stella said. “And what about Donny?”

She glanced in the direction of the interview room where the robber was still waiting.

“The crime he told us about checks out. There was a robbery last night at that address, and the items that were stolen match up. There’s camera footage too. So let’s hand him over to the local detectives. They can press charges and re-arrest him. Let’s go and wait for Richard in the meantime.”

As they reached the entrance of the New Haven police department, a sleek, dark Mercedes SUV pulled into one of the open bays outside. The man who climbed out was tall and fit and looked to be in his late thirties. He saw Stella and Maxwell and walked quickly over to them, looking stressed.

“Afternoon. I’m Richard. I’m here to meet the FBI,” he said.

“We’re the FBI. Agents Maxwell and Fall. You spoke to me earlier,” Maxwell said. “Shall we speak inside? It’s cold out.”

“Sure. Sure.” Richard followed them into the police station’s lobby and they moved to a quiet corner.

There, Richard gave a deep sigh. “I feel like this can’t really be true. Mark and Diane were such good people. I’ve known Mark since junior high. We went to college together. We saw each other often, played squash twice a week. I’m really struggling to understand how and why this happened.”

“Do you have any ideas?” Maxwell asked.

“Well, of course, I’ve been checking off all the scenarios I can think of, but nothing makes sense. They didn’t have dangerous jobs.

They weren't suing anyone or getting sued. Hadn't had any recent break-ins where there could have been a repeat robbery. So that leaves random crime, which is even more worrying because it means our neighborhood is being targeted. Or am I wrong?"

He stared at them anxiously.

"We don't think it was random, but we can't rule anything out at this stage. Was there anything worrying Mark recently?" Maxwell asked.

Richard frowned. "No. Not at all. His work was going well and was busy. He and Diane were planning a skiing vacation next month. There were no issues that I know of."

"When's the last time you saw him?"

"Thursday. Our squash days are Tuesday and Thursday evenings. I actually messaged him early this morning asking if we could make tomorrow's game later as I had a work meeting. I can't believe he would have been dead by then. It feels surreal. I wish I'd been able to stop it. My wife and I were having pizza night with the kids yesterday. Meanwhile, my friend was getting murdered a few blocks away."

"How would you describe Mark and Diane's relationship?" Stella asked, wanting to explore the dynamic between the couple in case there was any friction there.

"It was good. Solid. They were a happy couple. I never saw them argue. They seemed to have a very calm relationship. I admit, sometimes I was envious." Richard gave a short laugh. "My wife and I have our moments!"

"Any money issues? Any problems with relatives?" Maxwell asked.

"No. No money issues. Mark was a high earner and I think Diane was, too. And no kids, of course; that meant more spending money," he said ruefully. "They didn't have family in the area. Mark's parents live in Africa and his older brother works there too. He manages a safari lodge."

"Was anyone jealous of them?" Stella asked.

Richard rubbed his chin.

"I guess, theoretically, someone could have been, just because they had such a good life. They had a life that anyone would be envious of. But, you know, nobody in our circle is doing badly. Nobody is struggling. There's no reason for any of us to envy what they had, because—well, we all have similar," Richard admitted.

"Can you see any possible reason for this? If you had to guess, what would you say?" Stella asked.

Richard shrugged. "My thoughts keep on coming back to it being random. Which is the worry, as it's really freaking my wife out. That's why we agreed that I should drive over and speak to you, to find out if there is any information. You know, this kind of thing is disturbing. Makes one think we should be living in a gated community. My wife wants us to move."

"When we uncover more information, it should help you make a decision. In the meantime, thanks again for coming here to talk to us," Maxwell said.

Stella felt grateful that Richard had taken the time to speak to them, but his words only confirmed what everyone else was saying. The Taylors were well liked, and had no conflict or issues with anyone.

As Maxwell wrapped up the interview, Stella glanced toward the precinct entrance which she'd been checking regularly.

This time she saw the tech hurrying in carrying what was probably Diane Taylor's phone. She dashed over and intercepted him.

"Hey there, Agent Fall," the tech said. Stella smiled gratefully at him, recognizing him from other cases he'd helped on. With his ponytail and the tattoos on his arm, he looked more like a hacker than an expert who worked with law enforcement.

"I've deactivated all security on it, so it will open immediately for you," he said. "Hope it helps. We are still working on the other phone, and it should be ready within the next few hours."

"Thank you," Stella said.

She took the phone and headed straight to the back office. Richard's words were still fresh in her mind, and Stella was curious to see whether the communications on Diane's cell confirmed this friend's opinion.

Opening the slim, silver phone, Stella thought how strange it was to be handling an item that had so recently been used by a murder victim. She felt as if the phone must surely be a conduit to the thoughts and the hidden life of the user. After all, people lived on their phones in today's world. And as she'd learned, even married couples had their secrets. She wondered if Diane had been hiding anything away here, despite Richard's insistence that she and Mark had been the perfect couple.

At first swipe, there was nothing amiss. Diane hadn't made many calls over the weekend. She'd made quite a few during business hours earlier in the week. After noting down all the numbers so she could check up on them, Stella turned her focus to the messages.

There were communications to and from Mark. They were short and to the point. Diane didn't use emojis. Clearly, nor did Mark. Perhaps they weren't that type of people, being busy and pressured and career focused. At any rate, the messages seemed to be friendly enough, although brief.

There were a couple of messages to her mother, and a few work-related chats.

It all looked normal until Stella reached the conversation with a number saved as "Henry Flooring" far down on the list.

She opened it and stared in surprise.

All the message in this chat had been deleted, apart from the first one, which read: *"Hey there! Are you Henry who does the wooden flooring? We have a room that needs doing!"*

"Now why would this be?" Stella asked, curious about what the rest of the conversation had been, and more importantly, why Diane had deleted every other text.

Scenarios flitted through her mind as she puzzled over how to find out—quickly—what these had been and whether they were relevant to the case.

They might still be archived by the service provider but that would take a few days to obtain. Of course, Henry might not have deleted them and might still have a record. But she needed to find out more about Henry first.

Cradling the phone in her palm, Stella tried to think what the reasons might be for Diane deleting these messages. There was really only one obvious reason and that would be so that her husband would not see them.

But if those messages had been important then perhaps there was a record of them elsewhere. Diane could have emailed them to herself. Or she could have screenshot the conversation.

Stella opened up the images file and scrolled slowly through.

Here they were. Sure enough, Diane had wanted to keep a record of them. Now, Stella needed to find out why they were important enough to screenshot, but too private to keep visible in the chat.

Intrigued, Stella scrolled through the shots of this mysterious conversation.

"Hey there! Are you Henry who does the wooden flooring? We have a room that needs doing!"

"Hey there. I sure am. Do you want me to take a look and quote you?"

"Yes please. We are number 5 Parkway Drive."

"Will 9 am Monday work? We can then do the job Wednesday if you accept the quote."

"Sure. I'll wait for you Monday to discuss."

Then there was a break in the messaging. Presumably Henry had arrived at the house and done the job, because the next communications were a week later.

"Hey there! Just checking you are happy? About everything??" Unlike Diane, Henry used lots of emojis.

"I'm very happy, yes."

"If you are, I am. I like to keep beautiful clients like you as happy as I can! Are you available for a site meeting Tuesday?"

"Sorry, Tuesday won't work for me. I don't need a meeting. I'm good with what you have done."

"Tuesday lunch time then? I can do you any time!"

"I am happy, thank you, Henry."

Stella narrowed her eyes. This sure as hell wasn't a standard business conversation. Henry's words were full of double-entendres and the tone was flirty. It looked like he'd been pushing for closeness and she had been backing off, wanting to keep things on a professional footing.

Feeling now extremely curious, she scrolled down to the next screenshot. And this was where the conversation became totally one-sided.

"Hey, Diane! Not sure that flooring's holding up! I need to check it! Let me know..."

"Diane? Why aren't you replying? Are you not enjoying this anymore?"

"Diane, I tried to call. And I'm going to try again until you answer. Don't think you can get away with this."

Startled, Stella read through the rest of the one-sided conversation.

"Diane, if you won't take my calls I am going to come around and see you in person. What the hell do you think this is? TAKE MY CALLS OR ANSWER ME BACK."

"ok then, f-u."

*"How can you treat me this way? You are so disrespectful, you b***. You think you can get away with this? I should slap you! How'd you like that? Maybe you'll find me at your front door tonight! You better watch out!!!"*

"Wow!" Stella said. That had escalated quickly.

Diane sure had let the wrong contractor into her home. This guy had turned into a psycho. These messages were disturbing. Stella could see why she'd deleted and screenshot them. Perhaps she'd been planning to take this further and get a restraining order. Or at any rate, seek some kind of legal advice.

Had Diane told her husband? Stella couldn't work out why the messages would have been erased. Perhaps she didn't want Mark losing it when he saw how she'd been harassed.

At that moment, Maxwell walked into the back office.

"Come here, quick," Stella said. "Something very weird happened between Diane and a contractor at their home. I'm thinking this guy got flirty and was rejected. Read through the screenshots. This guy's threatening her. And he's furious."

Maxwell took the phone from her and read through the messages. Stella could see exactly when he reached the stage where things had gotten nasty. His eyes flew wider, just as hers had done.

"So who is Henry Flooring?" he asked.

"That's what I'm wondering. Especially seeing his last message to her was only a week ago."

"A week ago." Maxwell nodded thoughtfully. "That timing is significant. Read the number out, please? Let's trace it and find out who Henry Flooring is and where he works."

Not only did this man have a motive for harming Diane, and possibly her husband, but Stella realized he would know the layout of the house, having worked there. The wooden floors were in the bedrooms. The family room was tiled.

Henry must have known where the Taylors slept, and might have found a way to get in.

CHAPTER TWELVE

Stella reread Henry's messages as Maxwell looked up the number. The threats were chilling. How could a professional contractor, representing a company, start escalating things in such a way with a client? Stella wondered, feeling horrified all over again.

"His name is Henry Grant. He works for Forest Flooring, which is a wooden floor company with branches all over Connecticut," Maxwell reported.

"Let's call head office and find out where Henry is today," Stella said.

Maxwell was already picking up the phone.

"Hi. I'm looking to get hold of Henry Grant," he said, sounding innocent. "Is he in today? We're eager to discuss something he quoted us on."

He waited, listened.

"Oh, seriously? Whereabouts?" He paused, and then said, "But we're around the corner from Valley Drive. What number is he at now? He might be able to come by after he's done there... Number twelve? Yes, that's very close to us. Can we call him direct or would you rather get hold of him on our behalf?"

He waited again. "Great. Thank you."

Maxwell disconnected and shook his head. From his expression, Stella knew he was pleased to have the information so fast, and yet at the same time worried by the level of trust that would allow a receptionist to give out a home address to a total stranger with only the most basic trickery involved.

"Well, he's at number twelve. Let's take a drive there," he said.

*

When Stella and Maxwell pulled up outside Twelve Valley Drive, she saw the residents were busy with major renovations. The gates of the large, two-story home were open, and three vans were parked outside the triple garage. The front door stood wide and from inside,

Stella could hear the sound of hammering and drilling as she approached.

Two contractors were at work in the hallway, she saw, looking inside. A housemaid in a black uniform was keeping an eye on them, while also cleaning up the dust.

"Good afternoon," Stella said loudly over the noise. The men stopped what they were doing, and turned to stare at her inquiringly.

"I'm looking for Henry Grant," she said. "I understand he's working here today? We contacted head office and they gave us this address."

"That's the wooden flooring guy, right?" one of the contractors asked.

"The boards are being replaced in the family room," the housemaid said. "But why are you here?"

"We're FBI, ma'am," Maxwell said. "Investigating a crime committed in Parkway Drive. We're seeking information. You're not in any trouble," he reassured her, because now she did look worried.

She might be heading for trouble, Stella thought, if she was supervising a killer working in her employer's home.

"I guess you can come in," the housemaid said.

Stella and Maxwell walked in, and carefully navigated around the work taking place in the hallway. It looked as if the hall was being retiled and plastered. They teetered across a series of wooden planks, laid over the half of the room where the tiles hadn't yet been set in place.

Then the housemaid walked down a passage, which looked to be freshly tiled, and into another room that was still a work in progress. All the furniture had been removed from this room, which had huge windows and French doors overlooking the pool. Inside, two men were at work.

"Henry Grant?" the housemaid said. The man closest to them, who was sawing a wooden board, looked up inquiringly.

Maxwell stepped forward. "FBI Agents Maxwell and Fall," he introduced them. "Mr. Grant, we need to ask you some questions. It's in connection with a murder."

Stella took stock of this suspect. Henry was tall, well-built, and looked to be in his early thirties. With his dark hair and strong jaw, he was a good-looking guy. Briefly, Stella wondered whether he'd felt entitled to whatever he wanted, thanks to his looks.

Henry's first expression was of utter shock. Then, speedily, fear took its place.

"What is this about? I don't know what this is about! Why are you even here?"

The other, older man working with him put down his hammer and watched uneasily as Stella spoke.

"The victim is Diane Taylor," she said quietly.

Henry went very still. Only his eyes moved, his gaze darting in every direction. Stella could sense the panic surging inside him.

"That's terrible. I'm very sad to hear it. But I don't know anything about that. We did a job for her a couple of weeks ago. That's it. I don't know why you're here!" he repeated angrily.

The other man shifted uneasily.

"Look, I—I'm gonna go outside and take a smoke break. Okay?" He said the words to nobody in particular and then walked out through the French doors, glancing back in concern before disappearing around the corner.

"Jeez, I don't believe this! How did you even know I was here?" Henry was seething with righteous wrath. "I'm at work! On a job. If it doesn't get finished, we're in trouble. The homeowner wants it done by end of day tomorrow."

"Yes. I think you could be in trouble, but not because of this job," Stella said steadily. "Because of what happened between you and Mrs. Taylor."

Henry shrugged dramatically. "You need to start chasing someone else. I didn't have anything to do with this. I didn't even know about it until you arrived."

"Oh, yes. You knew."

"Why do you say that?" But now she heard the guilt, clear in his voice.

"You sent her a whole series of messages. The content is incriminating enough for us to bring you in. You didn't get what you wanted and then you started threatening her."

"Oh, jeez. Look, I don't know what went down there. But it wasn't anything to do with me. Nothing! I did a job at her house! That's the start and the end of it." He almost shouted the last word. His hands bunched into fists.

"That's not what we picked up from the messages," Stella insisted. "We picked up that you were propositioning her. You flirted and she cut you off, and when you didn't get what you wanted, you got angry."

There was a resounding silence in the room.

"Is that what you think happened?" Henry said, sounding incredulous.

"It's what I know happened," Stella shot back. "Don't try denying it. The messages are clear. The threats were screenshot on her phone. In black and white."

She waited for Henry to crumple in the face of this irrefutable evidence. But he folded his arms in a defensive way.

"You don't have the full picture. Not by a long road," he insisted.

"What is the full picture?" Maxwell asked, sounding at the end of his patience with Henry arguing back.

"You want it, I'll give it to you." To Stella's astonishment, Henry now also sounded irate. "Diane Taylor was no saint."

"What do you mean?" Stella asked, shocked.

"Sorry to speak badly of her, but to save myself I'll tell the truth. She called me in to do a job. She flirted with me in a way that left no room—and I mean no room whatsoever—for misunderstanding. We slept together the day after I finished the job."

Stella blinked in shock. This was a scenario she'd not considered at all.

"How did that happen?" Maxwell said, sounding as disbelieving as she felt.

"She called me back saying we needed to work through a snag list. There was no snag list. Only her, in her underwear, in the spare room. And then—then, yes, after that she cut me off and I pushed back, wanting more, and I got angry when she ghosted me. So that's what is missing from your equation and your theory," Henry concluded heavily.

With a jolt, Stella realized that actually, this explanation made sense based on the changing tone of the messages.

Also, Henry's version explained why Diane had not laid charges against the flooring contractor. That was something Stella had wondered about from the start, and now she saw a reason.

Diane couldn't, because she would have had to admit to the affair and Mark would have found out. That explained why she'd deleted the entire conversation from her phone. She had kept the screenshots but had clearly not taken any action.

"Do you have proof of this?" Maxwell asked harshly.

"I threw the condom away," Henry retorted in an angry voice. Then, as if trying to get a handle on his own emotions, he said, "My partner outside, who doesn't know a thing about what really went down, thought that I was leaving to check a snag list. You can ask him. And I have the record on my phone of when she called me, personally, to tell me about this so-called list. She did all her flirting in person or on a call. It was just me who was stupid enough to message." Henry sighed. Then he stared at them with the anger gone, and only a defeated appeal. "I'm working this job because my business went belly-up. I declared insolvency and they are paying me under the table. I've lost everything and if I lose this job, I have nothing. I promise I'm not lying to you, but if you don't believe me, and I get arrested, this could destroy me all over again."

Stella could hear the desperation in his voice. But Maxwell was intent on taking this all the way.

"Where were you on the night of the crime?"

Henry frowned. "What night was it? What time?"

"Last night. Give me your timeframe. I'm the one asking questions," Maxwell said.

"I—I got back home at seven last night. I went for a run. Then I went back to my apartment and got changed. I walked to the bar down the road. I got to the bar soon after eight. The barman's name is Evan and he can confirm I was there. I had a couple of beers, ate a meal. I talked to a few of the regulars, and to Evan. I was back home at about ten-thirty."

"Where's home?"

"Home is a one-bedroom apartment in northern New Haven. The bar is down the road from it. I don't own a car anymore. I don't have a luxurious life, Agents. I barely have any life. I'm paying, big-time, for the business mistake I made two years back, and now it looks like I'm going to be paying even more after sleeping with a woman who actually showed interest in me after all this happened and my life fell apart. Yes, I was angry. I should not in any way have sent those messages. Would I do it again? No. I was an idiot. I was emotional. I took it out on her because there was a lot to vent."

Henry was breathing deeply. He blinked tears away.

Stella felt he was telling the truth and that this story was genuine. She could see Maxwell now, reluctantly, thought likewise.

"Give me Evan's number, and the name of this bar, so we can confirm it," Maxwell said, in a resigned tone.

But Stella already sensed this story would check out. Devastatingly, Henry was not their suspect. However, he had given them important information. The Taylors were not the perfect couple. Diane had cheated with a contractor, and this raised questions about everything they had been told so far.

She headed, flat-footed, to the door.

"We won't make this public, assuming your version checks out," Maxwell said grudgingly. Before he turned away, he added, "But if you make a habit of threatening people in this way, you'll get yourself in trouble again, and next time, it might be worse. What you did was out of line. Unacceptable," he emphasized, glaring at the tearful contractor.

Only then did Maxwell turn and leave.

Even though Stella felt disappointed, knowing there were fault lines within this seemingly perfect relationship had given her a new direction to follow.

"I know who I want to speak to next," she muttered to Maxwell as they left.

CHAPTER THIRTEEN

Maxwell headed back into the New Haven police department, bowing his head against the cutting wind as he rushed inside. He felt crushed by disappointment, and was starting to panic that they were all the way back where they had started in this investigation.

The only progress they had made was to rule out strong suspects who had proved to have unbreakable alibis.

He'd driven past the bar on his way back and had confirmed Henry had been there last night. Camera footage had confirmed him there for the stated time. He would not have been able to travel to the Taylors' home and commit a murder.

Maxwell knew Fall had rushed off to check another theory, but he couldn't think of any other personal angles to explore. Not until Mark's phone was available, anyway.

That meant he had to go back to the other possibility, which was that this had been a serial killer crime. With no similar case history in the area, Maxwell would have to widen his search to look for any related murders.

The forensic tech who'd worked at the crime scene was sitting in the back office when Maxwell entered, compiling his report. Seeing him there made Maxwell remember the double murder he'd told them about, where the vase had been stolen.

He decided that even though the cases were not identical, it was worth following up on, if only because both scenes had been so clean and both murders so violent.

"Hey there, Govett," Maxwell greeted the man, whom he knew slightly from a previous case.

Govett looked up. "Hey, Maxwell," he replied.

Maxwell scooted into a chair on the opposite side.

"I'd like to know more about that case you mentioned when we were at the crime scene," Maxwell said.

"Sure. Why? You think there's a connection?" the man asked curiously. "It was a while back. Close to ten years."

"I know." Maxwell grimaced. "We're out of leads. This is a tough one."

Govett nodded. “I guess the lack of trace is a shared factor. Maybe there are more common elements. If I recall, it was never solved and went into the cold case archives in Delaware. The FBI office there might be the best place to contact.”

“Thanks,” Maxwell said.

He headed over to a spare desk and called the Delaware office.

“I’m calling to find out more about a cold case,” he said.

“Hold on.”

In a few moments, Maxwell found himself speaking to a brisk, competent-sounding woman.

“Agent Cachero,” she said.

“This is Agent Maxwell from New Haven. I’m looking to find out more about a case that happened nearly ten years ago and went cold. It was a double murder, husband and wife, and a silver vase was stolen.”

“Yes. I remember that case,” Cachero said. “I was put in charge of reviewing it a couple of years ago, but there was no new information to be found. It’s still unsolved. However, the vase was found, were you aware?”

“It was?” Maxwell asked, feeling shocked at this unexpected twist. “Found where?”

“A few months after the crime was committed. There was a heat wave, and the pond in the park a few blocks away dried up enough for the vase to be visible. Someone saw it and pulled it out and we traced it back to the robbery.”

Maxwell was stunned by this information.

“So robbery wasn’t the motive at all?” he said incredulously.

“It doesn’t seem so,” Cachero agreed. “It was just dumped. Either to make it look like a robbery at first glance, or else for some other reason, who knows what.”

“We have a very similar case here,” Maxwell said. “A double murder, and a valuable Fabergé egg replica was stolen and dumped on the street.”

Agent Cachero paused.

“Well, that is interesting,” she said thoughtfully. “That’s definitely a common factor. But the other case was so long ago.”

“Even so, we’re short of leads this side, and I’d like to look into it.”

“I’ll send you the file, if you like? It would be nice to put this case to bed, too.”

“Thanks,” Maxwell said.

"It's not copied yet. It's too old to be digital. So I'll need to do it for you. Can you give me an hour or two? I'll send it as soon as I can."

"Thanks. I really appreciate that." Wondering if he might ask more of the helpful Cachero, Maxwell tried his luck.

"One other thing," he said.

"Sure," she said.

"Are you in contact with the agents who handle cold cases in other states? If this crime was repeated elsewhere, there might be other records in other archives."

"I can find out," she replied. "It'll take a while longer, but I'll send out some emails and ask."

"Thank you," Maxwell said.

As he disconnected, Maxwell felt grateful for her help. It was an outside chance, but at this stage, he was willing to take any chance.

And the vase being found? That put a whole different light on the case and the potential links.

"Perhaps it's symbolic," Maxwell muttered to himself, wishing that the twisted logic of a killer's mind could be more easily unlocked.

Fall was the best person to do that. He couldn't wait to tell her about this new discovery.

His phone rang and he grabbed it, wondering if it was Fall on the line. But as he looked down at the caller ID, Maxwell saw to his consternation that it was his ex-wife, Brigitte. Or rather, his soon-to-be ex.

He closed his eyes briefly, suppressing a surge of frustration.

Calling during work hours was something they had discussed many times over the years, both when Maxwell was working his high-pressure job in IT, and when he'd joined the FBI after separating from her. He'd explained that it was often impossible for him to take personal calls during working hours and that she should message him instead, and only call if there was an emergency.

Of course, there could be an emergency. Brigitte's increasingly volatile behavior made those odds exponentially higher. She could easily have gotten herself into some sort of trouble and he couldn't ignore this call.

Sighing inwardly, Maxwell picked it up.

"Rick!" Brigitte's voice was high and stressed and he felt his stomach clench in anticipation that there was a terrible crisis.

"Is everything okay?" he asked quickly.

"I'm not well," she said in a trembly voice.

Not well. That could mean anything but he decided to start with the most obvious explanation.

"Your meds. Are you taking them?"

"My meds are not helping me!" Fury resonated in her tone, the emotion that made Maxwell's blood pressure skyrocket. "You think that shrink was doing me any favors by putting me on that poison? I refuse to take it any longer. I skipped my dose yesterday and I am going to throw the tablets away."

"Brigitte, no. Please, you need to rethink this decision. They are helping you." Maxwell felt as if he was trying to talk her down from a high ledge. If she took the plunge, she would risk not only damaging herself, but others, too. His frantic thoughts veered immediately to Fall.

"They're not helping. I don't need the meds. I need you!" Maxwell sat up in consternation at her words. "I need you. Come home now. Come back to me. I'll only be okay if you're with me."

"I can't. Brigitte, not during work. If you need someone to sit with you for a while, I'll come after work. But that might be late. It will be much better if you can call Dr. Benson in the meantime. Make an emergency appointment for this afternoon. I'll pay for it, no problem. That will be the best solution."

Maxwell did his best to keep his voice soothing and calm, because any hint of emotion would only trigger the vulnerable Brigitte. But it was too late, he realized. She was triggered already.

"You're not going to come and see me because you are with that other bitch! I know where you're going to be after work. I know she stole you away from me."

"You and I have been separated for more than a year," Maxwell began, but Brigitte was past the point of listening to any logic.

"Stop lying to me! She stole you and now I'm suffering. You have ruined my life! If you won't do it, then I'm going to fix this, and make sure she stops interfering! We need to be together again. You know how much I love you, Rick!"

Abruptly, she disconnected, leaving Maxwell feeling frazzled and emotionally wrung out from the short call. Things were going from bad to worse. If she didn't take her meds, Maxwell knew, Brigitte could be capable of anything.

He would have to warn Fall now, because one thing he'd learned about Brigitte was that when she made a promise like this, she kept it.

At least, with her erratic behavior and the threats she'd made, he now had everything he needed to make a clean break from her. And he could start the process of getting a restraining order against her as soon as they had wrapped up this case.

But would a restraining order be enough, he worried, or would she just ignore it, and stay hell-bent on doing as much damage as she could?

CHAPTER FOURTEEN

After leaving the site where Henry and the flooring contractors were working, Stella headed back to Parkway Drive, where the murder had occurred. She stopped opposite the Taylors' home and walked to the front door of Graham Haddow's house.

When she rang the bell, he opened it almost immediately.

"I saw your car pull up outside," Graham said apologetically. "I've been watching the street a lot more than I used to after this happened. Probably a lot more than is good for me."

"I hope you feel safer soon," Stella sympathized. "In the meantime, could I come in? I have some more questions."

This time, they were going to be harder questions. She was going to pressure Graham for the truth, because she suspected he hadn't told it all last time.

"Sure, sure. Some neighbors dropped off cookies for me earlier. Would you like some? And I can make coffee."

Without even waiting for her to say yes, Graham bustled through to the kitchen and got busy.

Stella let him work, not wanting to ask the questions while he was distracted. It felt surprisingly comfortable in the warm and cozy kitchen, as Graham pottered around placing the cookies on a plate, taking the coffee off the brew, and pouring cream into a china jug.

"I apologize for being fussy," he said. "I don't have too many visitors these days, and I want to get everything right."

"No problem," Stella said, feeling oddly soothed as she watched the ritual of the coffee making.

"There we are," he said, looking satisfied. "Let's go and sit down."

Stella took the jug and Graham carried the tray through to the family room. There, he invited her to sit, poured the coffee, added cream, and passed her the cup, together with the plate of cookies.

She took one and had a crunchy bite, enjoying the sweetness on her tongue. Graham was definitely a lonely man, she decided. And maybe she was lonely, too. Certainly she had never had a friendly father figure in her life. Not since the age of ten, at any rate. It was comforting in a way she'd never expected.

But she wasn't here for comfort, Stella reminded herself. She was here to probe deeper into what this man really knew.

"You were good friends with the Taylors," she said, putting down her cup.

"Yes, I was." Graham sounded confused, as if he wasn't sure why Stella was repeating information he'd given her already.

"Being so close, they would confide in you, correct?" Stella asked.

Graham's eyebrows shot up. "Confide in me? No, no, we were not that close. Neighborly. Not that close."

Pressing on, Stella continued. "Were you aware that Diane had an affair a while back?"

Graham pressed his lips together. For a few moments there was silence in his house. Stella didn't take her eyes off him. She knew he was going to be feeling the pressure.

He looked down with a defeated sigh.

"It feels wrong to give out personal information at such a time," he admitted in a low voice.

Stella felt a mix of relief and exasperation. He had known. If he'd said something earlier, it would have helped them a lot. But at least he'd admitted to it now.

"We need this background," she appealed.

Graham cradled his cup in his hands.

"Yes. Diane did confide in me about it. I think she saw me as a father figure, and she got quite chatty when we were alone together. She didn't explain the full circumstances. But she said that she felt ashamed of herself. Things were difficult, so she sought comfort from a stranger, was what she said. She'd done it once before, a year ago, and she did it again recently."

"Why were things difficult?" Stella asked.

Graham shook his head. "I don't know. That, she didn't say. I guess every marriage has its ups and downs. If I look back on mine, there were times I felt that way, too."

"And her lover from a year ago, were they still in contact?"

Graham shook his head. "From what I understand, he lived in Germany and was here on a contract. He went back to Germany a while after the affair ended."

"No other affairs?" Stella asked.

"Not that she told me about."

"Are you sure, Graham? This is desperately important. Affairs can lead to disasters like double murders. So if there were any other times when Diane cheated, please don't keep it from me."

"No." Graham sounded surer now. "I wasn't told about any other problems of that kind. And I encouraged Diane to seek counseling. I don't know if she took the advice, but she said she would."

"How do you mean?" Stella asked.

"I told her that something like that needs to be addressed. I advised her, very strongly, that she should put her cards on the table, tell her husband everything, and seek help. She thanked me for the advice and said it would be the best decision, that she was eager to get past this rough patch. She really loved Mark."

"Okay."

Stella picked up her coffee cup again, thinking over what Graham had said. There had been no other affairs to his knowledge. Since Henry had an alibi that Maxwell was busy confirming, Stella decided she could rule out anything from Diane's side.

But there was still Mark's side. She didn't know as much about him yet. They hadn't even gotten his phone back.

Her next step, Stella decided, would be to go to Mark's workplace. With a high-pressure job and spending a lot of time in the office, that would be the best place to find out more about what had been going on in Mark's life.

Given that Diane had had at least a couple of affairs, she felt sure that the relationship between the two of them was far more complex than anyone had first thought.

And couples had secrets. They'd found out Diane's secrets. Now they would need to uncover Mark's.

*

Mark Taylor worked for a large firm of chartered accountants called Heath & Jackson, with offices in many of the major cities statewide. The company had its own building in downtown New Haven—a gracious, double-story office with Georgian architecture, located opposite a park.

As she headed to the reception area, Stella noticed the parking lot was almost full. Heath & Jackson was clearly a busy firm. Inside the building, a wide reception desk was manned by three women, each wearing headsets. They were fielding calls and typing furiously on computer keyboards.

The closest one to the door was a pretty brunette with a short Afro hairstyle.

“Afternoon. Can I help?” she asked.

“I’m here to ask some questions regarding Mark Taylor,” Stella said. The brunette nodded, her smile vanishing.

“Are you police?” she asked.

“FBI,” Stella explained.

“His offices are upstairs. His secretary is Lillian Norman and his personal assistant is Cara Willoughby. I’ll call Cara now and tell her to meet you. You’re welcome to go upstairs.”

She indicated a gracious spiral staircase on the opposite side of the lobby.

Stella walked upstairs and at the top was met by a woman of about forty. Her platinum hair was pulled back in a bun, and her face was filled with stress.

“I’m Cara Willoughby.”

“Special Agent Stella Fall,” she introduced herself.

“Is there any update on this? We are absolutely traumatized.”

“We’re working on it around the clock, and hope to have answers soon.” Stella knew the standard response would offer cold comfort. Even she didn’t feel reassured by her own words.

Cara led the way along a carpeted corridor with doors at intervals. Most of them were closed but Stella picked up the muted trill of phones and the murmur of voices from inside.

Cara walked all the way to the suite at the end of the corridor. Inside, another reception desk stood empty.

“This is where Lillian usually sits,” Cara said. “She’s the secretary shared by Mark, and his colleague Daniel. She took time off today. She went home when she heard the news as she was too upset to work, which I understand. I worked exclusively with Mark. Please come through and I’ll try to answer any questions you have.”

She headed into a grand corner office that had a view over the large park. The enormous mahogany desk looked neat and tidy. The tall leather chair behind it, unoccupied, dominated the room with its presence.

Cara took a seat at the small, round boardroom table in the corner and Stella sat down with her here. Stella thought she looked twitchy and worried and stressed.

"What work did Mark do here?" she asked.

"Mark was a partner in the firm. He dealt mostly with our big corporates. We have a lot of corporate clients. He dealt with a few of the law firms, and two of the big chain stores. Daniel dealt with the other chain stores and also with two state departments that we do work for."

This didn't sound untoward or suspicious, but it was a good idea to make sure.

"Anything controversial? Any problems with his work?" Stella asked.

Cara looked blank for a moment.

"There are always problems. It's a very complex, high-pressure environment. We deal with problems and issues every single hour of every day. But I guess that's not what you are asking."

"No," Stella agreed. "I'm really wanting to know if there were any serious problems. Angry clients. Any clients with financial problems. Also, any clients who might have engaged in illegal activities?"

Cara shook her head. "No. I do know there are firms who handle those types of clients, but not us. We don't need to and in any case, we do a lot of work for government and state institutions so our reputation is important. We always vet clients carefully because we know how much business we could lose if we took on the wrong one. The clients belonging to Mark and Daniel are all listed companies or government institutions at this time."

"And work-wise? What was Mark's relationship with his colleagues?"

"Normal. I mean, the odd clash, of course, but nothing that couldn't be resolved with

a two-minute phone call. Nothing more serious than that," Cara said.

"Did he work closely with Daniel?"

"Not more closely than with any of the other partners because they had separate clients. They were both extremely busy, all the time. They used to joke the only time they got to catch up was in management meetings."

"Anything else you can think of? How did Mark seem in the past few days?"

"As normal," Cara said. "I mean, now I'm looking back, I'm stressing that maybe I missed something. But I really don't think so."

"Okay. I think that's all I need from you," Stella said. "Can I have Lillian's number, please? I'd like to give her a call and go to her place later."

"You need to do that?" Cara looked surprised.

"Ma'am, it's a murder investigation. We have to look into every single person who spent time with Mr. Taylor," Stella explained.

Privately, she thought that the secretary might be more willing to tell the truth. Mark's assistant could well be downplaying anything she knew about, especially if it involved the company. Interviewing a different staff member, especially on her home turf rather than on the work premises, might get a better result.

"Sure. I'll give you Lillian's number." Checking her own phone, Cara read the number out.

"Thank you," Stella said.

She decided she would call Lillian as soon as she was in her car. She headed out of the grand office buildings and back to the busy parking lot.

She climbed into her car, but before she could dial Lillian's number, her phone started ringing. It was Maxwell on the line. Quickly, she picked it up, hoping that he might have made progress.

"I have some news," Maxwell said.

"What is it?" she asked hopefully.

"The Delaware case wasn't really a robbery. The vase was dumped in a lake nearby."

Stella's eyes flew wide. This now meant there was a very distinctive parallel in the two cases.

"That's a big coincidence," she said. "So big, that it suddenly doesn't seem like a coincidence at all."

"I've asked for the case file to be copied and sent and I've asked if there are any other historic cases in other states that are similar."

"This could be a very important direction for us to go in." Stella had veered away from the serial crime theory. Now, she felt encouraged this line of investigation might be the way forward.

"There's something else, too." Maxwell hesitated and the tone of his voice chilled Stella even before he spoke again.

"I need to explain it face to face," he confessed. "It's personal, and it's potentially bad. I'll tell you when you get here."

CHAPTER FIFTEEN

Stella saw Maxwell waiting for her outside the New Haven police station. Clearly, this personal news was not suitable for sharing inside.

She felt nervous and upset. This must be to do with his wife. She hadn't wanted to hear her name, or any mention of her. Not after the destructive arc their relationship had taken over the past few weeks. Not when it felt like they were slowly rebuilding again.

And definitely not while they were working on such a pressured murder case. She couldn't afford such a distraction. Neither of them could.

She knew how focused Maxwell was on this case. So, if he wanted to tell her about Brigitte, Stella guessed it would be something that was really important and which couldn't afford to wait.

Maxwell's face looked tense as she approached. He took a deep breath, preparing himself, ready to get to the point and get it over with.

"This is not good," he said. "Brigitte is going off the rails. She's refusing to take her meds. She's blaming you. She is promising some sort of payback and she usually does what she says she'll do. In fact, she might know where you live already, or else be finding out," he said heavily. "She needs a restraining order, and I'm going to get that organized as soon as we're done with this case. In the meantime, if she threatens you directly, or confronts you, or causes any trouble with you, please tell me."

Stella's thoughts flashed back to the incident earlier.

"I think someone was watching me this morning in the basement parking garage," she said. "I didn't see who it was. I assumed it was connected to the Marshalls."

Maxwell shook his head, looking angry and upset. "Damn it, Fall. This is very disturbing. I don't know if it was her or not. She didn't mention that to me, but of course she wouldn't."

"What does she want you to do?" Stella asked.

Maxwell shrugged. "There's no logic to what she wants, apart from that she is trying to force me to cancel the divorce proceedings. But what about you and your safety?"

Stella made a face. "I've been under threat for a while. Don't worry about me. Let's solve your issues. Would it help if you go to her now? Sit with her for an hour, while she takes her meds again?"

Uncomfortable as it was to discuss this, she realized it had to be done.

"No," Maxwell said firmly. "It's not about the meds. Not at all. It's about her having a say in my life again. Having control. The meds are an excuse. Unfortunately an effective one, but if I go to her this time then I'll go every time. I can't allow it. St—" He stopped himself immediately but Stella knew with a clench of her stomach that he'd been about to call her by her first name. Personally.

"Fall, I can't allow it. I've offered to pay for an emergency shrink session. I said I'd come by after work. But I can't go there now."

"I'm sorry this is happening," she said. "Thanks for warning me."

"I'm sorry too. More than you know," Maxwell said in a heartfelt tone.

They gazed at each other, and the expression in his dark eyes made her heart beat suddenly faster. It felt the same as it had the time they stood together near her apartment, just before they kissed. Stella forgot for a moment that they were outside a busy police station, standing on the sidewalk in the cold.

Then she dragged herself back to reality.

"The sooner we can solve this case, the sooner you can sort this out. So, while we wait for the cold case file, is there anything else we can do?"

"Yes, there is. Mark's phone just arrived. It's been unlocked, so we can look through it."

With the personal conversation off the table now, Maxwell headed back inside and they returned to the desk in the back office which they were using for this investigation.

Stella sat down and swiped through the phone, glad to have something other than Brigitte to focus on.

Mark had been a nonstop message sender. She saw conversations between himself and Richard, the squash buddy who'd spoken to them earlier. There were multiple calls, especially during work hours. Stella knew it would take some time to track all those numbers and work out who they were from. The messages were quicker.

"You know, there's a lot of chatter here between him and someone whose name is only saved as L," Stella said. "But what's interesting is that it doesn't seem to make a whole lot of sense."

"Explain?" Maxwell asked.

"Take a look. This is a message chain from three weeks ago." Stella passed the phone over for him to read the confusing exchange.

"L, is the 13 available?"

"Sure thing."

"When can you hand it over?"

"6:30 @ mine?"

"Anything from your side?"

"CabS"

"See you then."

"It's weird, right?" Stella said. "Could be just a business message though? Could L be Lillian, the secretary? That would make sense, asking her if something was available?"

"There's something about it that sounds a bit underhanded, somehow," Maxwell said. "L? Like he couldn't save her full name?"

"Yes. I agree with you. The 13, what's that? A date? A kind of form? And CabS?" Stella glanced inquiringly at Maxwell. He was the one who'd been a forensic IT specialist in his previous life. Surely he had knowledge of accounting lingo.

"I don't have the faintest idea what it means," he confessed.

"Let's find another. There are a few of these." Frowning now, Stella took the phone back and scrolled further.

"McNs 430?"

"Private?"

"Yes."

Stella looked up.

"My first guess would be that this is Lillian. Let me check if the number's the same. I got her number from the office." Quickly, Stella referred to her notes and nodded. "Yes. This is Lillian. She wasn't at work today after hearing about his murder, so I think we take a drive to her place and question her right away. My feeling is that either they were doing extramural business activities on the side, or else they were having an affair."

*

At six-twenty p.m., in the sleety darkness, Stella and Maxwell pulled up outside Lillian's home. It was in a spacious, well-kept apartment complex outside New Haven's downtown area.

Lillian's apartment was on the second floor. They climbed the stairs of the grand and stately building, which had pretty gardens outside and a treed courtyard.

Stella knocked on the door of apartment 202, wondering what Lillian's reaction would be when she saw them on her doorstep.

A moment later, the door was opened by a woman who looked to be in her mid-twenties. She was pretty in an understated way. Her hazel eyes and bobbed brown hair didn't immediately grab attention. On seeing Stella and Maxwell standing outside, her eyes widened and her mouth opened in surprise.

"Lillian Norman?" Stella asked.

"Yes, that's me. Good evening," she said, with a question in the words.

"FBI. We'd like to speak to you about your boss's murder. Can we come in?" Stella said.

"Oh, goodness. I'm not sure I'm ready to speak about that," Lillian said sadly. "I'm still really traumatized by the whole thing. I can't believe it."

"It will just be a few questions. We need the information to solve the case," Maxwell said, steamrollering over this attempt at evasion.

"Sure. Please come in," Lillian capitulated.

Stella walked into the spacious apartment. They sat down in the comfortable living room. As Lillian hurried around tweaking cushions and removing a coffee cup from an antique table with a faint air of panic, Stella revised her opinion of the woman's looks. It was only a few moments later that you noticed her porcelain skin, high cheekbones, and long eyelashes that gave her an air of haunting beauty.

There was no time to waste. The evening was closing in and this crime was still unsolved. Hopefully they would learn more while here.

"We opened Mark Taylor's phone," Stella told her.

"The phone? Oh?" Lillian said, her pretty eyes wide.

"There were some messages between you and Mr. Taylor," Stella said.

"The messages. Yes, he often used to message me on my cell," Lillian replied.

"The content was strange. It didn't seem like work-related communication."

"How do you mean?"

"I'm going to read one to you." As she read out the strange-sounding message, Stella kept a close watch on Lillian's reaction.

She was clenching her hands anxiously but Stella knew that on its own was not necessarily a sign of guilt. With two FBI agents in your lounge, anxiety was to be expected. Certainly, Lillian was holding her nerve and she wasn't looking ready to break.

"We communicated in a kind of shorthand," she said. "Mr. Taylor hated texting. He found it very time consuming. He liked to keep things short and so I learned to copy him and send things back to him the same way."

Hated texting? The hordes of other conversations on his phone didn't back up that statement, Stella thought.

"But what does that message mean?" she asked.

Lillian narrowed her eyes thoughtfully.

"It means he needed private documents for a client by four thirty p.m.," she said.

Stella couldn't find anything to pick on. It did make sense in a way. It was plausible—just. She still was not convinced though, and nor was Maxwell.

"Was Mr. Taylor involved in anything irregular at his work? Were you assisting him with anything irregular? I am asking you this with a warning. If you were, and you don't disclose it to us, you are going to be in serious trouble and you will face criminal charges. If you are able to assist us, then we will not pursue charges," Maxwell threatened.

"I wasn't assisting him with anything like that," Lillian protested and for the first time Stella heard a note of genuine honesty in her outraged words. "We were busy enough with our regular clients! I worked a fifty-hour week just helping him with our regular clients. We were turning away new business and handing it over to other accountants because we didn't have time. There was no reason at all to get involved in underhanded deals!"

"Then why the messages?" Maxwell insisted.

"It's how we communicated." Staying calm, Lillian shrugged apologetically.

"What does CabS mean?"

"Let me see the message again, please? I need to read it in context."

Stella wondered if the pretty young secretary also wanted to buy herself some time as she peered down at the screen.

"Ah. It's an abbreviation for one of our clients' holding companies."

"What's the full name?"

"Crowley, Henderson and Shell."

“That’s not exactly an abbreviation.”

“I understood. He understood.”

“Were you having an affair with him?”

“No. I’m not in a relationship. I live alone!”

Stella gazed around the apartment again. It really was a nice place. Far more luxurious than Stella herself could afford. Perhaps Lillian had family money, but if so, why was she working fifty-hour weeks as a junior secretary?

While Maxwell was struggling to make headway with his interrogation, Stella’s gaze rested on the well-stocked wine rack in the corner of the room. Thinking of the strange CabS abbreviation, she came up with another theory. A simpler and more plausible one.

While Lillian was focused on Maxwell, Stella continued looking around the room.

Now that she had a chance to focus on this space, she was realizing there were some surprising hints to be picked up.

For a start, on the drinks table in the corner, there were two glasses. And there were also two bottles. A sweet cream liqueur and an expensive cognac. Something about the arrangement suggested that two people might have enjoyed different drinks at the same time.

On the coat stand near the door was a ladies’ trench coat and scarf, but there was also a red silk tie, carefully folded, and a pair of black woolen socks that looked far too large and masculine to be used by the petite Lillian.

Why would these items have been left on the coat stand, so conveniently accessible? Stella wondered. The only reason was that there was a regular male visitor to the home.

If this was the case, it made sense to Stella why Diane had so impulsively embarked on the affair with Henry. And why she’d confided to her friendly neighbor that there were problems in her marriage. It was because her husband had been cheating on her with his secretary, and she must have found out.

Stella stood up and walked over to the coat stand.

She held up the tie, and saw Lillian’s eyes widen and horror fill her face. As Stella had expected, the items of men’s clothing had become so much a part of her everyday life that she hadn’t noticed they were out in full view.

“You live alone. But you and someone enjoy different after-dinner drinks. Is this the same someone who leaves his tie and his socks at your place, and you’re so used to him doing it that you put them on the coat stand, so he can grab them on his way out next time? Perhaps if we went through to your bedroom we might find even more proof? A spare toothbrush in the bathroom, men's shirts in the closet, a charger for his phone on his side of the bed?"

Lillian's mouth opened and closed. Her face had flushed a deep pink. Stella felt pleased her guesses were accurate.

"If we're going to admit that someone does come by your place regularly, then from those coded messages, I'm pretty sure it was your boss. CabS stands for cabernet sauvignon. That's my guess. Am I right? If I'm not right, who do these belong to?" Speaking sternly, she placed the tie back where she'd found it, next to the socks.

Lillian looked around in a panic. But faced with the proof, and drilled by Maxwell's furious gaze, she capitulated. Her eyes filled with tears.

"He—he used to come around to visit me. He rented this apartment for me because it was close by. We used to adore each other's company. That was all. It wasn't sexual," she insisted.

Stella saw Maxwell literally roll his eyes at this unlikely protestation of innocence.

"Did he promise you more?" she asked Lillian.

"He mentioned that when the time was right, he would leave his wife for me."

"Did you believe him?"

"Yes. I did believe him. For a while, anyway. Recently, I changed my mind."

Stella took another look at the attractive woman. She was not tall, but she was fit and lean. Her arms were toned. Stella guessed that in a fury she would have been more than capable of beating Diane to death. And perhaps the romantic involvement also explained why she couldn't bring herself to deliver a killing wound to Mark.

"So he promised you something and then strung you along. How did that make you feel?" she probed, hoping to delve into Lillian's deeper motives.

Lillian shrugged. "I was getting frustrated. I was getting angry."

"Angry enough to kill him?"

"No!" Lillian exclaimed.

"Really? Being lied to is very hurtful."

"I know it is!" The words exploded out of her. "Of course I know! And I wanted to hurt him!"

"So how did you hurt him, then?" Stella felt poised on a tightrope.

"I didn't kill him! I didn't!" Breathing hard, Lillian jumped to her feet and faced up to her. "If I'd been a different person then I might have. But I knew I could hurt him a worse way."

"How?"

"By quitting!" Lillian's face twisted in angry triumph and Stella heard Maxwell let out a huff of surprise. "I knew that would break him. He never thought I would leave. He relied on me for so much. So that's what I was going to do. That was my revenge. I can show you the emails. I was sending my resume out and I already had interviews lined up. I will forward you the evidence!"

This was a good comeback. But it wasn't the emails Stella was interested in now, but rather Lillian's alibi.

"Where were you last night?"

"I was with my mother. That's our cards and dinner night with her and my sisters. She lives in Torrington. It's a long drive so I always sleep over."

"Do you have proof of that?" Stella asked, wishing every twist and turn of this case wasn't ending in disappointment.

"I can get proof," Lillian said anxiously. "Her street has a boomed entrance with cameras, so they do have a record of the cars coming and going. I left there at six this morning and drove straight to work to avoid the traffic. I was at work by seven a.m. Then we got the news of the murder at about nine and I left immediately."

"Give us the name of the street and your mother's address. And the details of your car," Maxwell said.

"Sure. Sure, I will. I'm so sorry I didn't tell you this upfront." Apologetically, Lillian complied. "I thought it would complicate things and I was really worried that I might get into trouble and that people might think I had something to do with it."

"Next time, be truthful!" Maxwell sounded seriously angry. "You've been wasting our time. We have a murder to solve."

As soon as Lillian had scribbled down the information, Maxwell took it and marched out. Stella followed him.

"Well, if this checks out, we're heading to another dead end," Maxwell snapped. "Both of them were cheating, but neither affair caused serious consequences. Since we're all out of leads—again—we should probably call it a night."

It was now after seven p.m. The sleet was turning into fluttering snow.

"I guess we had better get some rest," Stella said in a disheartened tone.

But as she spoke the words, she felt a chill. Her apartment wasn't a safe place anymore. Her private space was being watched.

She knew that at this particular time, she might be in more danger inside than she had been out on the streets during the investigation.

Maxwell must have sensed her fear, because he said, "If you don't want to be alone—with things so difficult right now, do you want to sleep at my place? I'll take the couch," he said hurriedly.

"It's okay," Stella said, reflexively refusing the offer. Part of her longed to accept it, to spend the night in the safe haven of his place, but there were way too many complications, starting with his jealous wife.

"I'll be fine," she reassured him.

She wasn't even convinced by her own words. Worriedly, Stella realized she was sounding exactly like Viv. But at least Viv had agreed to go somewhere secure for the night. Stella wasn't doing anything so sensible. She would be sleeping at home.

CHAPTER SIXTEEN

Stella climbed out of Maxwell's car at the entrance to her apartment building. He'd insisted on dropping her at home. She knew he was worried about her. She was worried, too, but also felt uneasy about the memories that were surfacing of the last time she and Maxwell had been in a car together, outside her place.

They'd both gotten out, because she'd had an injured hand. He'd helped her to the door and on the way, they had ended up kissing. It had been their first kiss. Also their last, as it turned out. Stella didn't want to think about the emotions she had felt as events had unfolded later that night. The misery. The betrayal. The ripping apart of her hope and trust. Nor did she want to think again of that heart-pounding moment when their lips had touched. How it had felt. How she'd responded to him.

"Thanks for the ride," she said in a formal voice. Embarrassingly, she was one hundred percent sure that Maxwell's mind was also fixated on that disastrous kiss. But he also wasn't admitting to it. He replied, equally formally, "See you in the morning, Fall."

That was it. She was out of the car. Just before she closed the door, she heard his voice, sounding pleading. "Hey, Fall?"

She couldn't turn back, not now. Not when she was ninety-nine percent sure that he was going to ask her again to stay over at his place.

And that, this time, she wasn't sure she had the will power to say no.

Turning her face away from the gusting snow, she walked inside. The elevator beckoned but she headed to the stairs. That was her fitness rule. Always the stairs up to the fifth floor, even though her legs were already tired from chasing down Donny at the station earlier.

Pushing open the door to the stairwell, she felt distracted by the emotions that had surged as she'd said goodbye to Maxwell. Had it been the right thing to do? Should she have accepted the offer? Did his wife have a key to his apartment? If Brigitte did, then it would definitely have been the best decision to stay away.

As the door banged shut behind her, Stella had only a surprised moment to pick up that it was very dark in the stairway and that the overhead light on this level was not working.

And then, in the gloom, from behind her, a hand grabbed her hair.

Stella shrieked as she was yanked backward. In the sliver of light that filtered through the door from the lobby, she saw the gleam of a sharp, triangular blade.

A box cutter. Her stunned mind took in the lethal shape even as it flashed down to her.

Ducking as fast as she could, Stella kicked out at her captor, punching behind her, desperate to avoid the bite of that razor-like blade which now, in the dark, she couldn't see at all. She yelled again as her hair was tugged so hard she felt strands pull agonizingly out of her scalp.

Kicking back again, Stella made contact. Her shoe hit the bony length of someone's calf and she heard a gasp and felt the attacker flinch away. But he—or she—didn't let up on their hard, tight grip.

She had to try and free her hair. She was trapped, her head twisted back in agony, and aware that the length of her neck was exposed and vulnerable. Pulling her head to the side, she gritted her teeth against the pain, trying to protect her neck. She needed to turn around and face her attacker. That would allow her to fight more effectively.

But the hold was too tight. She didn't have any idea who was trapping her this way, but the grip felt strong and powerful enough to be a man's. He was clutching the blade in his right hand. She glimpsed it again as he lunged behind her. Gasping, she thought it would reach her this time. Flinching away, she managed to grab his sleeve just in time.

The blade ripped through her jacket's shoulder. She felt the tug and heard the tearing of fabric. An inch to the left and it would have stabbed straight into her neck. Now all she had was a grasp on a loose sleeve. It wasn't enough, he could still reach her.

Her breath was coming in fast, rough gasps. Fighting for her life, she flung herself backward, hoping to avoid the blow she sensed as much as saw. But all that happened was that he tugged on her hair harder. In white-hot agony, Stella recoiled, knowing she was exposing her throat again. But by twisting around, she found another chance.

She stabbed backward with her left elbow, putting all her force into it. And she got him in the gut.

The painful shock caused him to double over. Gritting her teeth, Stella tugged her hair free. Finally, his clinging grasp loosened and she was able to jerk her head away.

He still had the knife. She had to get it away from him. Just one slice with that blade could open up an artery. Take out an eye.

Suppressing her visceral fear at being on the receiving end of that lethal blade, Stella turned, ready to meet her adversary head to head, already planning where, and how, she would attack to cause maximum pain. She needed to take him down before he could regroup and use that knife again.

But he'd clearly decided that having lost the element of surprise, the fight was over. To her astonishment, even as she turned, he slammed himself against the lobby door. Light flooded in as it burst open. Without looking back, he raced across the lobby and out of the apartment's main door.

Rushing after him, hoping to get some physical details, all she could see was that he was wearing black. Black jacket, pants, gloves, and hood. She hadn't glimpsed his face and would never be able to pick him out of a line-up.

"Watch out!" Stella yelled, as the man came face to face with another woman walking in. She had visions of that lethal blade being used and felt frantic that someone else might suffer the consequences of her having escaped him.

To her relief, he didn't use the knife. He just pushed the elderly woman viciously back, so that she skidded on the icy sidewalk, slipped, and fell. Her purse flew across the paving and her shopping bags scattered to the ground.

Reaching the entrance, Stella hesitated.

She could chase the killer or she could help this woman.

There was no choice. He—she was sure now it was a man—was taller than her, would be faster, and had a head start. Already, he was racing to the street corner and disappeared around the side of the building. By the time she got there, she suspected he would be long gone.

Just as he had known her habits and had a clear plan for ambushing her, she was sure he had an equally good plan for making his getaway. Especially since, if things had gone the way he intended, he would have left a corpse behind.

Stella was shaking all over as she helped the shocked, tearful woman to her feet and collected her bags. Her scalp was burning. Her neck ached and her shoulders were throbbing from the life-and-death struggle that nobody else had seen.

"Are you sure you're alright?" she asked the elderly woman.

"I—I think so." She took a tentative step forward. "Nothing seems broken," she said in relief.

As she handed the woman her purse, Stella's thoughts veered anxiously to Viv.

If this man was sent by the Marshalls, Viv could be in danger. Even now, he might be on his way to her to attempt the second part of his mission.

"What happened? Did that man try to mug someone?" the woman asked, as Stella quickly placed the groceries back into the bags.

"I'm not sure," she said. "He's gone now. I'm sure you'll be fine. Shall I ride up with you in the elevator?"

"Yes, please. I'm on the fourth floor."

Carrying one of the bags, Stella walked inside with her and pressed the button. The ride up to the fourth floor seemed endless. The doors opened and Stella handed her the bag. The woman walked out.

"Thank you again, my dear. You stay safe, too," she said, before turning and walking carefully down the corridor.

The doors closed again.

As soon as they had shut, Stella pulled her phone out and began looking up Viv's number.

When the elevator opened on the fifth floor, she rushed out. Her pulse accelerated in fear as she checked the corridor, but it was clear. Then she rushed along it, turning the corner that led to her apartment, second-to-last in the row.

Glancing down, she switched her phone to speaker.

The call connected and began ringing.

The corridor was empty.

Stella arrived at her front door. It hadn't been tampered with and looked just as it had when she left that morning.

Listening to the phone ring and ring, feeling consternation flare inside her, she dug in her jacket for her keys. This call was about to ring through to voicemail. Viv wasn't picking up.

She realized she'd never been to Viv's home. Although she knew she lived somewhere in Greenwich, she had no idea where, and couldn't rush there to help her.

As she took the keys out, Viv answered and Stella felt a torrent of relief that was so powerful her legs literally felt weak.

"Stella. What's up?"

Stella fumbled the key into the lock. Turned it. The door swung open.

Her apartment was quiet. There was nobody inside.

Quickly, she turned and locked the door.

"I've just been attacked, Viv. Are you okay?"

"What?" Viv sounded incredulous. "Me? The question should be, are you?"

Stella had also locked her bedroom door before she left that morning. That door was still locked. She checked the bathroom, glancing inside. It was all safe. There was no more threat. For now.

"I'm okay. It was someone with a box-cutter knife. I'm worried they might come after you next. Where are you now?"

"I'm home. I just got in. I arrived back ten minutes ago. I locked the door immediately and now I'm upstairs, packing a few things before calling a cab." Viv sounded breathless. Clearly, she was rushing to get out of her house.

"Please, be very, very careful. Call the police now. I know you don't want them with you all the time, but they need to be there when you go out to the cab. They'll do that for you. Ask Detective Bradshaw, or else tell them you have his permission. You need to take every precaution now."

"Thanks for the warning. I will," Viv promised her. "But what are you doing tonight? I feel very concerned about you, Stella. You want to come with me to this place? I can book another room for you, no problem."

"I'm going to stay here. I'll call the police and let them know what happened as soon as I've got everything locked up."

"You think you'll be safe enough?"

"There's a chain on the front door and I'll put a chair under it, and I'll lock my bedroom door and put a chair under that too. They can't reach me then without making a lot of noise. The noise will warn me, and I'll keep my gun with me."

Viv paused.

"I guess that sounds like the best option," she agreed. "Take care, and we can speak tomorrow. I'll let you know as soon as my lawyer and I have left the police station."

"You take care too," Stella said.

She ended the call. Unlocked her bedroom door. It was quiet in there. Nobody waiting. So most likely, this attacker had been working solo. Even so, she knew he might be back. She would need to keep on high alert tonight.

Preparing for a sleepless night, her heart still pounding and her ears straining to pick up the faintest sounds from outside, Stella began dragging chairs into place to fortify her apartment for the dangerous hours ahead. As soon as she felt safe, she would call the police and tell them what had happened. But she had little confidence that they would be able to track down a killer who seemed to have planned so well, especially since his hood would have concealed him from the only camera in the lobby, which was mounted on the ceiling near the elevator.

They had tried once and she knew they would try again. The Marshalls would not stop until they had achieved their aims.

CHAPTER SEVENTEEN

Viv paced around her bedroom, picking out the clothing to pack in her overnight bag. She was going to take enough for two nights, she decided, just in case there was a delay in Gordon Marshall's arrest. It would be better to hide away in this safe retreat, rather than make herself vulnerable where she knew they could find her.

It was surprising how Stella Fall's words had stuck in her head. Even though she'd protested against them, she realized their truth.

She was going to be in danger. She'd known that deep down even before Stella had called her now, with tension twanging in her voice, to say someone had attempted to murder her.

Viv picked out underwear and socks. Two spare shirts. What else? The countryside spa where she was going was extremely secure and discreet. They catered to many celebrities, and wealthy clients post–cosmetic surgery, and she knew they would not give out guest details no matter what. And, because of this clientele, the place was very secure.

She added yoga pants to the pile. They had a gym there. It would do her good to take a class and relax, and feel like she was back in normality for a few hours. She'd felt very far removed from her normal life for the past couple of weeks.

Walking to the bathroom, she packed toiletries and cosmetics into her bag, hoping she was bringing along everything she needed because her brain was not working as it should, due to the stress. She had always been sharp and never absent-minded, but now it felt as if her mind was like a sieve. Randomly, important things just vanished from it, giving her a huge fright when she thought about them again and realized they'd been forgotten.

The one thing she had made sure of, though, was to check the front door was locked, with the chain in place. She'd done that the minute she had arrived home and had turned around to check it a second time, and make sure.

Shoes! There you go. She'd nearly forgotten to take a spare pair of shoes. See what stress did?

Quickly, Viv picked out a pair of casual shoes and walking shoes and added them to the bag.

She heard a noise downstairs and her spine prickled. She froze, listening.

But it was just the heating kicking in. It always made the same noise, a strange thud that made her jump even when she wasn't fearing for her life. Now, it just about made her heart stop.

When she got back, she was going to get that switch fixed as part of the major security upgrade and overhaul she planned to do.

Viv zipped her travel bag closed. Time to go. The only item still to collect was the manila envelope with all the information inside. This was the information that would bury the Marshalls. Destroy them. After what she'd been through and what they had done to Fall, Viv felt a vengeful pleasure at the thought. They deserved it.

She had left the envelope on the hall table when she walked in, and would pick it up and put it in her purse on the way out.

It was getting late, and this place was a half-hour drive away. She'd better hustle. Especially since she had to call a cab still. Or maybe she should take her own car. Viv hesitated.

It would be convenient to have her car there. But cars could be followed, even tracked. She knew this and although she had no idea how the Marshalls might have done such a thing, Viv had to admit there was a lot they had done recently that she hadn't believed them capable of.

Besides, she'd promised Stella, and Viv tried hard to keep her promises.

A cab it was, then.

Quickly, she opened her phone and navigated, with some unfamiliarity, through the process.

Her ride was eight minutes away. That was irritating, Viv thought. But on the other hand, with current traffic conditions, it showed her that the trip would only take twenty-five minutes. So that balanced out.

She headed downstairs and into the hallway.

She looked at the hall table.

It was empty.

Viv felt her heart literally start to pound with shock.

The envelope wasn't there. How was that possible? She was sure, sure, sure that she had walked straight in and put it down on that mahogany table. The memory felt etched in her mind. She'd seen it lying there.

But she couldn't have. She must have put it somewhere else and now, with blind panic setting in, Viv had no idea what she could have done with it. The cab would be here in seven minutes and she had lost the most important item that she needed.

The one that would allow her to live her life again.

Her hands were cold and wet. She let out a shaky breath, trying to calm herself. Trying to think through the steps she had followed since arriving home, she remembered the route she'd taken. She'd locked the door, that she knew for sure.

Although, now doubting herself, Viv tested it. It was still locked and the chain in place. So wherever she'd put the envelope, it was inside the house somewhere.

Now she just needed to work out where. She'd gone into the kitchen first. She'd been thirsty and had wanted a drink of water. It was entirely possible, Viv reasoned, that she had taken the envelope with her in there, put it on the kitchen table, and just misremembered everything afterward.

This memory gap was so disorienting it felt as if her whole world had shifted strangely. With stress flaring inside her, Viv went into the kitchen.

The light was off. That had been another thing she must have done without thinking. She'd turned it on, she knew she had, because otherwise she would not have been able to take the glass down from the cabinet and fill it with water.

Reminding herself to double-check all the lights were off before she left, Viv snapped it on.

And let out a scream of fear.

There, sitting at the kitchen table, was Gordon Marshall.

Gordon smiled at her; the most evil expression that Viv had ever seen.

He was holding the manila envelope in his manicured hand. Wearing a gray business suit, he was clean shaven and his dark hair, flecked silver at the temples, looked perfect.

"You—you —" Viv's voice was faint and quivery. She felt sick with fear and her mind was reeling. She'd locked the door! She'd locked it and checked it.

The only answer was that Gordon had got in before she had arrived home. He'd found a way into the house and had hidden there, waiting for her.

Gordon had been inside all along.

"Perhaps you're looking for this?" he said, in that tone of his she knew so well, where seething anger was concealed by the flimsiest veneer of politeness.

How was she going to get that envelope from him now? All her efforts had been for nothing. Her plans were shattered.

"No, I—I'm not looking for anything," she stammered out, feeling unable to say anything sensible at all, and knowing that it was too late for any kind of pretense or misdirection. Gathering her courage together, she said, with all the strength she could muster, "What are you doing in my house? You had no right to break in here."

"I'm just a guest," Gordon said, the words icy cold.

Gordon stood up. He took a step toward her, and Viv saw he was holding a gun in his other hand. She realized, with a terrible fear, that this was no longer about the envelope. It was about her life.

"No," she whispered, her mind racing as she thought for ways out of her predicament.

The cab. The cab would arrive soon. If she could somehow keep him talking for another—another five minutes, then the cab would be here and if she was lucky, the driver might even come up to the house and ring the doorbell. At the very least, he'd call her.

Gordon raised his hand and Viv caught her breath as she saw the pistol had a long barrel-like attachment on the end.

A silencer, her terrified mind screamed at her, that's a silencer and he's put it on the gun so that he can shoot you now, without making a noise.

Then, feeling a sense of doom, Viv realized what else she'd forgotten.

Stella had implored her to call the police. She'd said it was essential they were there when Viv walked out of the house and went to her cab. The police would have been here by now if she'd done things the way she'd been advised. The police could have saved her now. She'd broken her promise, but only because she'd forgotten all about it in her fragile, fragmented state of mind.

Viv's nerve abruptly broke. She turned and began to run. Her only hope now was to get out of the house, flee him, get away as far and fast as she could.

But as she reached the kitchen door, she screamed again.

Another man was waiting there, black-clad, with a ski mask over his face.

He caught her, his arms powerful and his grasp impossibly strong. She couldn't fight it. He was putting something over her head, a black cloth. It was suffocating her, with a rank, chemical smell.

Viv gasped, feeling this choking substance getting dragged all the way down into her lungs. This was it. She felt consciousness escaping her. This was the end. They had won.

As darkness rushed over her, she wondered how she had ever fooled herself that they could lose.

CHAPTER EIGHTEEN

Stella sat bolt upright, breathing hard, scattering her covers. She groped for the gun on her bedside table, fumbling the grip into her hand as she stared around the gloomy room. Quickly, she snapped the light on.

She'd been sure someone was in the room with her. She'd sensed his breathing, and the almost imperceptible movements that the shadowy form had made as he edged toward her. She'd seen the gleam of his eyes in the muted light that filtered in from outside and she'd heard the distinctive creak the floorboards made under his otherwise quiet footfalls.

Fear prickled her spine at how intense, how believable, that short dream had been. It had been more vivid than reality.

But the room was quiet and the chair was still under the door handle. She could hear nothing wrong. No noises, no bangs or crashes. It was six-fifteen a.m. and she'd survived the night.

Stella climbed out of bed and quickly got dressed, ready for her day. Only when she was clothed and had her shoes on did she pick up her gun again, move the chair away from the door, and cautiously open it.

The other chair at the front door was in place, too. Apart from herself, her place was empty. Nobody had broken in or tried to and she was alive and unhurt.

She let out a long sigh of relief.

Now that she felt more reassured about her own safety, Stella turned her focus back to the problematic case. Despite a long, tough day of work yesterday, they were no closer to discovering who had killed Mark and Diane. The case was stalled and she knew that Roth would be unhappy with their lack of progress.

Stella got coffee on, remembering with a sudden smile how Clem had always told her that in his opinion, the FBI was basically fueled by brainpower and caffeine.

Thinking of Clem gave her an idea. Perhaps she should call him and bounce some ideas off him. Clem was fascinated by serial killer cases. And Stella was starting to become more and more convinced that this had to be a serial, because they had found no other link between the victims and any of their connections who could have wanted to murder them.

But, as she picked up the phone, Stella decided that this time she was not going to be completely honest with her mentor. She wasn't going to tell him that she was in serious danger and that there had been another attempt on her life yesterday. She didn't want Clem to know that. It would worry him needlessly.

She jumped as the coffee machine let out a steamy hiss, and then sighed. Living on her nerves was the way it would have to be. At least it would keep her alert to danger.

But she was going to keep that troubling knowledge to herself and make sure she spoke only about the case, Stella decided.

She poured coffee into her cup and added cream, feeling reassured by the normality of these everyday actions. Then, sitting at her dining room table, she called Clem.

He answered briskly.

"Stella Fall!"

"Clem. I hope it's not too early to call you?"

"Never too early. But I was about to call you. I'm here in New Haven to give a seminar. It starts at nine, so I have a couple of hours to spare. If you don't have to be at work immediately, how about we meet up for an early breakfast?"

"That sounds great," Stella said. In fact, she couldn't think of anything more welcome than a face-to face with her mentor right now.

"Message me your favorite local place. You know the area better than I do by now. I can join you in half an hour," Clem said.

*

Walking up to the table where Clem sat in the coffee shop down the road from her apartment, Stella felt amped to see her mentor again. Although they'd spoken frequently, they hadn't met in person since last September, when he'd arrived at the FBI Academy and whisked her away to New Haven to help with an urgent case.

As soon as the rangy, gray-haired man saw her, he leaped to his feet with a grin. He looked fit, well, and crackling with vitality. He'd joked he was even busier in retirement, which he'd taken a few years ago at the age of fifty-six, than he was when he'd been working for the Bureau, but Clem thrived on adrenaline and activity.

She was sure that as she shook his hand—Clem wasn't a hugger—he was also remembering the first case he'd gotten her involved with here. After all, it was the reason she had received a job offer from Roth. That case had defined her future.

But every case affected her present, Stella remembered uneasily.

Coffee was already on the table, she saw.

"I ordered us breakfast. Eggs, grilled cheese, fruit. Thought it would save time because I'm sure you're busy. But why did you want to talk?" he asked as Stella sat.

"I'm looking for a different perspective. We have a difficult case on the go, Clem. A suspected serial. It's my first one," Stella said. "A couple was murdered in their home. It was a very violent crime. The killer beat and stabbed them to death. There's absolutely no one personally connected to them who is raising any red flags as a suspect."

Clem pressed his lips together and gave her a sympathetic nod. "Serials. The toughest cases there are. I guess you had to come across this at some stage."

"I know. But even taking into account that it might be a serial crime, I feel we have exhausted all options. I'm just not sure where we can turn next. We've looked at all their connections. We've researched historic crimes in the area. There's a link to a past crime, but that was ten years ago."

"Nothing else since?"

"Not that we know of. We are widening the search to see if there's been anything in other states, but nothing has come back yet. I feel helpless. This case is generating so much fear. Everyone in the neighborhood is panicking, wanting to move. And we can't come up with answers or solutions."

Stella felt frustrated all over again by how helpless they were.

But Clem was staring at her sharply.

"It sure is generating fear," he observed. "You've checked over your shoulder four times already since you sat down."

With a rush of shame, Stella realized she had inadvertently been looking behind her far too often for the observant Clem not to notice.

"Is it just the serial killer you're worried about?" Clem asked. "Or is it something else? If it is, tell me."

Sighing, Stella realized she would have to spill the truth to her perceptive mentor.

"The Marshalls are out to get me," she said. "Someone attacked me in my apartment's stairwell last night. They had a box cutter."

Clem's eyes widened as Stella continued, feeling cold at the memory of the shock and fear.

"I got away, but whoever it was managed to escape. They are still out there and could try again. And I'm not the only one in danger. Viv, the Marshalls' family friend, is trying to put a stop to this. She has information she thinks can take them down. But they are so well connected, I'm sure they will find out she's gathering it. I'm worried they will manage to stop her from getting it to the police in time."

Her thoughts strayed to Viv. This morning, she should be meeting with her lawyer and the police. Stella hoped it would go smoothly and that Viv would stay safe.

Clem shook his head. "That's such a tough situation. I know how you must feel. I'm extremely concerned that they are using violence. You can't live your life when you're being targeted by a hit man, and you can't do your job, either."

"I'm trying," Stella protested.

"I'm sure you are. But it's not the sensible solution. You should tell your boss about this and go into a safe house, or under police protection. At least until this Viv gets the information in front of the police."

Stella shook her head.

"I can't do that, because what if there are more delays? I might end up being there for weeks. And I definitely can't do it now, when I'm handling such a serious case. I can't let my partner down. Or disappoint Roth."

Clem sighed, pressing his lips together and looking resigned, if troubled, by her refusal to look after herself.

"Well, I guess the only advantage to the situation is that the more they try to harm you, the more they expose themselves and create a trail of evidence. And the more likely it is they will slip up and do something that you can use to put them in jail for life. But that's a minor benefit, given that the risk to you is completely disproportionate."

"I'm trying to manage it," she insisted.

"Stella, you will not be able to do this on your own," he said seriously.

"How do you mean, Clem?" she asked.

"Please, ask for help if you need it. In a situation like this, it will be your connections and your relationships that can save your life. I'm not exaggerating. If you refuse to take additional safety precautions, then use them."

Clem sounded as serious as she'd ever heard him. Stella nodded, feeling scared all over again by the reality of her situation, but grateful for the advice.

He added, "I know you're a proud, independent person, but there is nothing wrong with asking for help when it's your life on the line. You have people who care for you. I'll do anything I can to make sure you are not in danger."

"I will do that," Stella promised.

"And about the case, you have to remember, it's just another murderer at work. The same as what the Marshalls are trying to do. Serial killers seem to be machines. I know that's the feeling when you are up against them and it's deeply demoralizing. But they are not."

Stella thought about what Clem had said, feeling her way through his logic. She felt her mind leap at the challenge as she realized where her mentor was going with this advice.

"You mean, the little details will bring this person down? That's what you're saying, isn't it? That he might be a psychopath but he's only human and he will have made a mistake somewhere along the line?"

"Yes," Clem said. "Somewhere along the line, I absolutely guarantee you, this person has slipped up. He's made an error. Go back, Stella. Check again, confirm everything, relook at this every step of the way. I guarantee you that you will find something you overlooked. That's how I solved one of our most difficult serials twenty years ago. Just by going back over the facts, again and again, until I found all the loose ends. The small details that you wouldn't think to check. And I relooked at those until I found the error he had made. And that I had made in turn, by not examining the evidence closely enough."

Stella nodded thoughtfully. "Thank you so much for the advice, and the points you've made. We're all only human. I guess our own mistakes can also add up. I can already think of a couple of areas where I could go back and relook at what I've done," she admitted.

Clem nodded in approval. "Now you're getting it," he said.

Stella checked the time. "I'm getting a ride into work today, and Maxwell will be outside my place in ten minutes. We've got a massive amount to do today, so I'd better go. I don't want to delay him," she said.

"It's been great seeing you. But one other thing, Stella," Clem said as she stood up.

"What's that?" she asked, because he sounded grim now.

"It might feel like redundant advice with everything else you're going through, but I'm going to give it to you again. Don't trust anyone. These killers are dangerous and they're often far more intelligent than we'd like them to be. You're tracking him, but don't be fooled into thinking you're the only hunter. He might also be tracking you."

CHAPTER NINETEEN

Stella rushed down the street after her early breakfast with Clem, and was waiting outside her apartment at eight a.m. when Maxwell pulled up. She had to admit that after the breakfast spread, two cups of coffee, and Clem's companionship, the day seemed brighter. They might not have caught the killer, but having a direction to pursue made all the difference.

"Everything went okay last night?" were his first words to her.

"Not really," Stella said.

"Why?" Maxwell stared at her, now looking seriously worried.

"Someone tried to attack me in the stairwell." Stella had to confess the facts to her case partner. Much as she didn't want to, she knew that any attempt on her life could represent a risk to him, too.

"Fall! What happened?" Maxwell swallowed, adding hesitantly, "Are you sure it was the Marshalls and not Brigitte, trying something violent?"

"I doubt very much it was Brigitte," Stella explained. "This person had a box cutter. I am pretty sure it was a man. About five-nine, five-ten. Wiry. Strong. I managed to fight him off and he fled out through the main entrance. I imagine he had a getaway plan in mind and was just actioning it."

"Hell. That's serious. Why didn't you call me? Did you call the police?"

"I didn't want to worry you. I just wanted to hole up in my apartment and keep away from any potential threats."

Maxwell nodded grimly as she continued. "I did call the police and I'm sure they will be there this morning to follow up with the property manager, but the guy was wearing a dark hood and I doubt camera footage will pick up anything. I didn't even get a clear look at him or see where he fled."

"What can we do to keep you safer?" Maxwell sounded even more anxious than Clem had done and yet again, Stella was reminded of her mentor's good advice to take help when it was offered.

"Maybe, for the next few nights, you could walk me up to my apartment. If they're watching me and they see you with me, they won't try to jump me again. Unfortunately they knew my habits and knew I'd take the stairs and be alone."

"Good idea." Maxwell sounded pleased to be able to help. "And I'll meet you in the morning and walk you down again. Riding to work and back with you would also help."

He pulled out of the apartment's street parking and started the drive to the New Haven offices.

"Having you with me would help a lot," Stella said gratefully. Clem was right. Allowing other people to support her was the right thing to do and she could already feel some of the stress she'd been holding was lifting away.

Even the wintry morning, though gray with cloud, seemed sunnier as Maxwell followed the route to the FBI New Haven headquarters. She enjoyed being able to take in the views on the way to work as he headed down State Street, where the FBI offices were located. There was the local train station coming into view. Beside it was an office tower, and she always enjoyed the sight of the ultra-modern, loft-style apartments beyond, which each had their own cool look and character. It felt refreshing to take in the details of the urban jungle where they worked.

Reminded of Clem's good advice, she told him what her mentor had said.

"I had breakfast with Clem just now. He flew in from Chicago."

Maxwell glanced at her. "He often gives you advice on cases, doesn't he? You've mentioned how you bounce ideas off him. Did you get a chance to do that?"

"I did," Stella said.

"And?"

"He said everyone makes mistakes."

"Explain?"

"The killer has made them. He's slipped up. We just haven't found the slip-ups yet, and that's because we have also been careless in not checking ourselves enough and following every single detail."

Maxwell let out a pained breath. "Ouch. That burns, Fall. I guess all the more because it's true. I know we must have overlooked stuff. In fact, I can already think of one thing I mentally diarized and never did."

"What's that?" she asked.

"It's the housekeeper. We never tracked her down or interviewed her. I'm going to make a start on that, and look for her details in the phone records."

"Good idea," Stella said.

"I also want to confirm the layout of the neighbor's house. Remember, Roger and Anthea said their bedrooms were out of earshot. I want to check that, and also find out if he can confirm the 'looking after the kids' story in more detail. Perhaps there's something he did, or someone he spoke to. Maybe he sent a couple of mails while he was with his children."

Stella nodded. "Yes. That will be helpful. I can think of a couple of issues on my side too, so I'll start from the first one I thought of and work my way forward."

"I guess we get straight onto that, then," Maxwell said.

"Yes. As soon as we get to New Haven, I'll check up on my case notes, and then take a car and head out."

"Just be careful," he warned, looking anxious again.

"I promise I will. I'm going to start with confirming an alibi."

Stella knew where she needed to go. She had never checked Graham Haddow's alibi. No matter how elderly and innocent he appeared, facts were facts and the correct processes had to be followed.

As soon as she had read through the case notes, Stella decided to go straight to the restaurant where Graham had claimed to be on the night of the murder.

*

Stella arrived at Amigos in the Beachview center just as they were opening their doors for the day. A waiter was setting out a specials board in the window. When he had it in place, he hurried over to her.

"Morning, ma'am," he said. "We officially open for lunch service at eleven, but if you want tea, coffee, or drinks, or a place to sit, we can help you now." He smiled.

Glad that this was a friendly place, Stella pushed on with her questioning.

"I'm actually here to check up on some facts. I'm an FBI agent investigating a local murder."

"Oh!" The waiter looked astounded. He looked her up and down all over again. "Wow. I guess that would be the couple who were murdered down the road?"

"That's correct," Stella said.

"Our customers have been talking about nothing else. And we knew them, too. They came here to eat occasionally. It's very disturbing."

"I'm looking to confirm all the facts we've been told. On the night of the crime, we were told that their neighbor, Graham Haddow, came here to eat. He's a middle-aged gent, maybe in his late sixties."

"Graham Haddow, Graham Haddow… I was working on that night. Why don't I remember him?" the waiter asked.

For a moment, Stella felt a surprising clench of her stomach.

Graham? A false alibi?

Then the waiter continued.

"Okay. I've got him now. He sat at the table in the corner and he read a book for a while. Gray-haired guy. He's often here on our specials night. We get a few retirees on those nights. They love the specials, so the place is always quite full."

"What time did he arrive and leave?"

"I can't remember his exact arrival time, but—let me check on the list."

The waiter walked quickly into the restaurant and headed to the reception desk, with Stella following. There, he paged back in a large, leather-bound book.

Okay, he didn't book a table. So most likely he would have arrived before seven to get a seat. And I can confirm what time he left. I'll need to look back on the table check quickly," the helpful waiter continued.

Turning to the till, he looked on the computer, scrutinizing the screen carefully as he scrolled.

"Table twelve, let me see." He nodded. "He asked for the check at nine p.m. I think he might have stayed another half-hour or so. He didn't rush away, definitely."

"Thanks," Stella said.

She was relieved to know that Graham had been telling the truth, although looking back on the timeline, she realized he had arrived home during the window of time when the Taylors had been murdered. But there was nothing she could do about that, Stella acknowledged. Alibis were often not perfect. However what she did need to do was confirm the rest of Graham's statement.

She walked outside to her car and headed back to the FBI New Haven head office, deciding she would need to base herself there for her research as it would involve accessing archives.

As she drove, Stella checked behind her frequently. Her thoughts strayed to Viv as she did so. She hoped her brave, blond ally had gotten to her meeting safely and that her evidence truly would hammer the nails into the Marshalls' coffins, and put them in jail once and for all.

She hadn't ever thought that Gordon Marshall could be so dangerous and vindictive.

He was a sociopath for sure, Stella decided, hiding his true character behind his well-groomed, confident veneer. But when it came down to it, she knew he was just as cold-minded as a serial killer was. Like them, he didn't hesitate to act without any conscience, and far outside the boundaries of the law.

Stella parked outside the New Haven offices. She hurried along the walkway to the main entrance and headed in, surprised by the sense of relief she felt as she stepped through the door. In this place, she would be safe. Nobody who wasn't FBI would get past the security checkpoint at the door without an appointment. Even then, they would have to go through a metal detector and provide ID.

She headed down the passage to Roth's offices. Walking in, she realized she'd be working solo as Maxwell was still out and Roth was nowhere to be seen. She remembered he'd said yesterday he was traveling for a series of meetings.

Sitting down at a desk, Stella accessed the archives. She hoped she would be able to confirm Graham Haddow's statement that he had moved to Connecticut a few years ago after his wife had died.

Scanning the archives, she saw that Mr. and Mrs. Graham and Harriet Haddow (née Richter) had lived in Ohio for fifteen years. But that was way back, Stella noted. Checking the information, she frowned. There was a detail out of place. What was it?

Harriet had died of cancer eight years ago, but Stella's eyes narrowed thoughtfully as she saw the deceased woman was referred to as Harriet Richter. Why was that? Had she been divorced from Graham before her death? That didn't add up with what Graham had told her. He'd never mentioned a divorce.

Even though this was starting to feel tedious in terms of detail, Stella reminded herself that tedious fact-checking was often what solved cases. This seemed like a tiny and insignificant fact, but what if it exposed a bigger lie?

She decided the best way to find out the full story would be to speak to one of Harriet's living relatives. According to the records, Harriet had a brother, Kevin Richter.

Hopefully, Kevin would know more, Stella thought, moving to yet another set of records as she searched for Kevin's contact details. Research was time consuming and she had learned from experience that if you lost focus for a moment, you ended up making a mistake or overlooking something important.

"Here we go," she muttered to herself, writing down the two available phone numbers. Hopefully, at least one would get her what she needed.

Stella called the first right away.

It was out of service. This happened. She had two chances and she'd just have to hope the other number worked.

At least it connected. Stella listened to it ring and ring.

After five rings, it was picked up. She heard a deep-voiced man on the other side.

"Kevin here," he said.

Relieved, Stella introduced herself.

"I'm Stella Fall from the FBI. I'm doing some background research following a murder. Is that Mr. Kevin Richter?"

"It is, yes." Kevin sounded surprised. "Why are you're speaking to me? What murder? I don't know anything about a murder."

"Two residents in Bridgeport, New Haven, were murdered two nights ago. Graham Haddow is one of their neighbors. As I'm sure you can understand, we need to confirm every last detail of every version in such a serious investigation."

"Of course," Kevin said.

"I noticed that your sister, Harriet, was referred to by her maiden name at the time of her death. I wondered why that was, and if she and Graham were divorced at the time?"

"Yes, that's right," Kevin said. "Harriet divorced Graham—oh, it must be eleven years ago. She kept their house in Mansfield, Ohio, and he moved away. She already had the cancer diagnosis at the time of the divorce, but she did better than anyone expected. She had been given a year at most, but she beat the odds and stayed relatively healthy for two more years. We lived just down the road from her and saw her almost every day. Then she deteriorated very suddenly and passed away."

"I am so sorry you had to go through that," Stella said. "Do you know the reasons for the divorce?"

"She wasn't happy in the marriage anymore. Between you and me, she said that Graham's behavior was becoming erratic. That he was no longer the man she'd married. She never really went into detail about it, but she said she felt she'd be more comfortable on her own and he didn't contest it. It was an amicable divorce."

"I really appreciate this information," Stella said.

"If you like, I can find out the address where he moved, and the exact date he left. I know I have it somewhere, because we forwarded some mail. I'll call you back when I've got it."

"That would be helpful. Thank you."

She put down the phone feeling stunned by this information.

Graham Haddow, the likeable man that she'd thought didn't have a dishonest bone in his body, had lied to her and fudged the timeline in his background.

Furthermore, he'd behaved erratically enough for his wife to divorce him.

Stunned by this bombshell, Stella decided she was heading straight back to Graham's place. She'd never thought of him as a suspect, never believed that this benign, gentle man could possibly be involved, but these lies were certainly painting a different picture.

CHAPTER TWENTY

Stella arrived at Graham Haddow's house feeling upset and conflicted. She was angry with herself for having missed such important details in a witness's version. And furious at herself for being too trusting. Climbing out of the car, she berated herself because she perceived this as a personal weakness that could have compromised this case.

She had seen Graham as a father figure and had automatically disbelieved he could be a suspect in this terrible crime.

Now, his lies and flawed behavior were uncovered, and she had some hard questions for him. If he didn't provide her with good enough answers, Stella decided she was going to bring him in.

There he was! Outside, gardening. He was digging up a flower bed on the east side of the house. A bag of soil lay nearby. A complex mix of emotions flared as she saw him.

"Agent Fall!" He scrambled to his feet when he saw her, hanging onto the windowsill for support as he struggled up. His face warmed with a welcoming smile and Stella felt briefly unsure again.

He didn't look guilty. He didn't look anything except normal and helpful. Looking at how he was clutching at the windowsill, she doubted he would have been physically capable of committing the violence that had played out in the Taylors' home.

But then, why those lies?

She headed over to him and spoke sternly.

"Mr. Haddow, we've been confirming a few facts in your statement."

"Go on?" he said.

"There are inconsistencies in your version."

He frowned slightly. "There are? How's that possible?" Now there was a note of panic in his voice. "I've tried my best to tell you the full truth! Please, tell me what you've picked up. Perhaps it will be easy for me to explain. I hope so. I'd hate for you to doubt me in any way."

"You told us that you moved here after your wife passed away."

Now, she saw Graham was standing very still.

"We checked this version and found that you divorced your wife before she passed away. The person I spoke to said that she asked for the divorce because you were starting to behave erratically. You never mentioned a divorce to us. You implied that you and your wife had been married up until the time of her death. You never told us your behavior had caused such serious problems."

For a moment, she stared directly into Graham's eyes, seeing his own, a pale, watery blue, slightly narrowed.

Then he let out a defeated sigh and lowered his head, staring down at the freshly dug soil.

"I should have told you the truth," he said softly.

"What is the truth?" Stella spoke loudly and she could hear she sounded irate. She was angry with herself and also with him, for not having lived up to the expectations she had of him as the kindly, reliable neighbor.

"This is hard for me to say," he said.

Stella wasn't weakening.

"It's been pretty hard for me to accept that a witness account is untrue. It actually casts doubt over everything you've said so far," she accused.

"When Harriet was diagnosed with terminal cancer, it broke me apart. I couldn't handle it. At all. She was the strong one. I had a nervous breakdown. I couldn't cope with the reality of what lay ahead. I am deeply ashamed of how I behaved and that I wasn't strong enough to support her. But instead, I fell apart, I was emotional, I had to go on medication and I was no help to her at all. My mental state was upsetting her and yes, it was shocking how quickly our relationship developed fault lines."

"Okay," Stella said.

She hadn't thought there could be a reason for this outright lie but she had to accept this did sound plausible.

"Eventually she suggested the divorce. She had a very strong support structure with her family. I agreed it was probably best for both of our mental health. We discussed it in depth and decided it would be best if I moved out of our home in Mansfield, and made a fresh start elsewhere. So that's what I did."

"And you didn't tell me this, why?" Stella said again.

Graham shook his head. "I can't begin to explain to you how ashamed I am of what I did. I don't tell anyone. None of the neighbors here know. Nobody I have spoken to since knows. You are the first person I have actually confessed this to." He took a deep breath and blinked rapidly. "I'm going to guess that you might have spoken to Harriet's brother, Kevin. I don't think Harriet ever told him the full story. I know that even with a terminal diagnosis, she wanted to protect me because he would have been utterly furious if he'd known how I'd let her down. And maybe she also wanted to protect herself from the stress of being caught up in a full-scale family war and having people say terrible things about the man she married. Things which I deserved," Graham said heavily.

"I understand," Stella said. She did, now. She could imagine how the pressure might have weighed too heavy on him at such a time, and made him unable to cope with the situation. Everyone had their breaking point and clearly that was his.

"I've tried to be a better person since then. Involved in my community. I give my time wherever I can. I feel like I owe her a debt. I'll be trying to repay it for the rest of my life," he explained.

"I guess none of us know how we will respond until a situation happens," Stella said. She wasn't going to show Graham that she was both touched and shocked by the explanation, which sounded to her very sad.

His flaws had destroyed his marriage and he'd been unable to support his wife at such a critical time. That was nothing short of a tragedy.

Her own parents' marriage had been flawed, too. Her mother had been unstable. Now that she knew more about her father's disappearance, Stella understood more about the possible causes for why her mother's instability had worsened over the years. Rhonda had been living with intense fear, stress, and loss ever since her husband had been forced to vanish. No wonder their mother-daughter relationship had been damaged.

"We never know how we will respond when the chips are down. Isn't that the truth?" he agreed.

Then he glanced at the sky, as if seeking to change the subject. "It looks like it's going to rain any minute, and I need to finish digging this bed. I think I set myself an overzealous challenge," he said, wryly.

He turned back to his gardening, picking up the bag, but as he lifted it, a corner slipped out of his hand. The bag thumped down on the grass and split in two, soil bursting out of it.

"Ouch," he said, putting a hand to his back as he straightened up slowly.

"Are you all right?" Stella asked.

"Yes, yes, I'm fine." Graham stared down at it and shook his head as if disgusted by his own weakness in every way. "Probably, I should have waited for the gardener."

"Let me help you," Stella said. She didn't mind getting some soil on her hands in the line of duty. Grabbing the edges of the bag, she lifted it up and cradled it in her arms, trying to keep as much of the soil as possible inside. It wasn't that heavy, she thought, and it brought home to her how cruel aging could be. Most likely, when he was her age, Graham could have lifted four such bags with ease.

She lowered the bag into the bed and stood up, brushing soil off her arms, surprised that she was enjoying the deep, rich scent of the mulch.

"Oh, thank you so much. That's such a help," Graham said. "I feel like a clumsy idiot. But it has to be done. I've decided I'm going to move, and I need to make this lovely home as pretty as it can be."

"Where will you go?" Stella asked.

Graham sighed. "I don't know. I loved this neighborhood. But perhaps it's time to move somewhere warmer. Florida has always been the place I thought I'd finally retire. It's been a tough decision to make. I don't think I do well with death. I didn't cope with my wife's death at all, and I'm not coping with this catastrophe, either."

"I'm sorry to hear that," Stella said, feeling bad for this likeable man who was not as strong as he wanted to be, either physically or emotionally.

He turned to her again. "Is there anything else I can confirm with you? I promise that was the only part of my past that I was untruthful about, but you probably doubt my whole story now. I'll gladly go through it all with you if you like."

Stella shook her head. Graham's alibi had checked out to her relief, and she was satisfied with the explanation he'd given her for why he had lied. It had little to do with wanting to withhold information from her, and everything to do with trying to deny his own personal failings that he was ashamed of.

"That won't be necessary. You've confirmed what I needed," she said. "It's not likely I will need to speak to you again, but if I do, please give me the truth, even if it's difficult for you."

Feeling regretful that he'd proven himself to be an unreliable witness due to his own weaknesses, Stella stared at him sternly until he gave a contrite nod.

"I will do that, Agent Fall. I promise."

Turning away, Stella noticed that the neighbor diagonally across the road from him, Anthea Parsons, was standing near her garden gate and looking expectantly at Stella.

Anthea looked as if she might want to speak to her. Wondering if she might have any new information, Stella headed across the road to their home.

As she got closer, she saw Anthea was frowning.

"Morning, Agent Fall," she said. "We spoke to Agent Maxwell just now. Now I see you're here. Is there any new information on the case?"

"We're working around the clock on it, but it's a complex investigation," Stella said, giving her standard response for "absolutely no information and we're feeling stumped." Clearly, Anthea understood what these words meant because her frown deepened.

"How can it be complex when good people were murdered so brutally?" She shook her head as if asking the question more to herself than to Stella.

"Did you confirm what you needed to with Agent Maxwell?" Stella asked, putting the ball back in her court.

"Yes. He called us a while ago and asked us to send through the house plans, and some copies of texts that Roger wrote while he was checking on the kids, on the night of the murder. We remembered he'd messaged some memes to his sister that night."

"Thanks," Stella said, feeling reassured that that Maxwell had been able to confirm with more certainty that Roger was where he'd said he was.

"But I saw you were speaking to Graham. Why are you questioning him again?" Anthea's gaze drilled her.

"I was confirming details in his version," Stella explained.

Her explanation didn't make Anthea any happier. Now she looked positively angry.

"Excuse me for being ignorant of the way things are done," she seethed. "But it seems to me you are spending far too much time harassing innocent people. I mean, we're parents of three young kids, and we have had to try and prove our whereabouts on a totally normal family night when we were at home. And sending through the house plans! For goodness' sake! It feels—it feels invasive. And now you're targeting Graham! He's such a kind person and he's badly traumatized by this. He told us so. It just seems that if you spent more time concentrating on finding the actual killer, you might get further!"

She shut her mouth and her face flushed red. Clearly, she felt shocked by her own outburst.

"I understand," Stella said calmly. There was no point in getting defensive. And sadly, Anthea was totally right that they had been spending time harassing innocent people. Every person who was a suspect or a witness or a neighbor who was not the actual killer would probably feel like they were being bullied.

Anthea sighed. "I'm sorry. That was out of line," she admitted.

"It's no problem. It's an extremely stressful situation," Stella said.

"We're moving," Anthea declared to her. "Roger has decided we're selling up and relocating to a gated community in West Haven. We haven't slept properly since this happened. Kids aside, because they're staying with Roger's sister for a while, he and I are both up several times a night now, checking our alarm, looking out the windows. It's no way to live."

Her words gave Stella an idea. Perhaps there was a potential angle that she hadn't yet followed. Previous neighbors.

She knew Graham was a long-term resident, but what if another neighbor of the Taylors had recently sold up, and then come back to commit a crime?

"How long have you lived here?" she asked.

"We've been here three years." She gave Stella a sideways look as if wondering whether that was the best she could do in terms of investigating.

Stella was wondering the same.

But, since all other avenues had resulted in dead ends, perhaps it was worth following up.

"Who are you using to sell your house? And who sells most of the homes in this neighborhood? I'm looking for a person who would know of any other houses that were sold recently in this area," she said.

"The answer to both is Bronwyn Hughes from Haven Realtors. She sells most properties in this area, although I don't think she'll find it the easiest job after what happened next door."

"Can you give me her phone number, please?" Stella asked.

"Sure. I can do that. Give me a moment." Anthea dug in her jacket pocket, took out her phone, and read the number to Stella.

"I'll let you know as soon as we've made any further progress," Stella said to the still-irate woman, before she turned back to her car.

Once she was safely inside, she called Bronwyn, who answered on the first ring.

“Bronwyn Hughes. How can I help?”

“This is Agent Fall, from the FBI,” Stella said. “I need some information on the neighborhood where the Mark and Diane Taylor were murdered. One of the neighbors said you have local knowledge and do most of the house sales?”

“Oh, yes, I do,” Bronwyn said confidently. Her voice sounded warm and friendly. “I’ve worked in this area, and for Haven Realtors, for a decade, and have so much local knowledge. Perhaps some of it could help you. Why don’t we meet up? I’m in the area now. Can I buy you a coffee somewhere?”

“That sounds great,” Stella said. “Please message me the address where you’d like to meet up.”

She felt hopeful that the knowledgeable real estate agent, with her excellent local knowledge, might be able to share something relevant to this frustrating case.

CHAPTER TWENTY ONE

When Stella arrived at the local coffee shop ten minutes later, Bronwyn was already seated inside, with two coffees ready on the table. She smiled as soon as she saw Stella walk in hurriedly, and stood up to greet her. She was a round-faced woman of about forty, with sparkling brown eyes and curly red-brown hair.

"Agent Fall?" she asked.

"That's correct."

Immediately, Stella could see she was a true people person.

"Come over here, sit down, sit down," she encouraged. "You're an actual FBI agent?" She sounded surprised and intrigued.

"That's correct," Stella agreed.

"Oh, my dear! I have so many questions! What a fascinating career. How long have you been with the FBI?"

"A few months," Stella explained.

"It's so good to see a woman agent. I love it when ladies do a job that's perceived as belonging to a man's world. I'm all about equality. But this case must be a big challenge for you. So terrible!"

"It is. We're looking at all angles to try and get information."

"Well, whatever I can do to help, I will. I don't mind admitting there have been a lot of people wanting to sell up in the past couple of days. I'm inundated with calls. Movement in the market is good for me usually, but not this time. If this case was solved, it would give new buyers a lot more confidence about choosing this neighborhood," she shared.

"I was wondering what recent sales there have been in the area. Particularly, homes close to the Taylors' residence that might have changed hands in the past few months."

"There have been a few recent sales. Let me check for you."

Putting down her cup, Bronwyn turned to a sleek silver laptop and tapped some keys.

"Let's start with a fairly close radius. In the actual street, or the closest crossroad?"

"That sounds good."

“Well, the most recent sale I remember without even looking it up,” she said, “that was the property two doors down from the Taylors’, on the cross street. Number eight Partridge Drive. He sold about two months ago.”

“Really?” That piqued Stella’s interest. That home was close enough that this resident could have interacted with the Taylors and had issues.

“Do you know what kind of a person he was? Why he sold?”

“He said he had tenant problems and decided to cut his losses and sell. You know, I always tell people, you cannot be too careful about vetting tenants. If you get the wrong one in, it causes months of heartache, as it’s often not the easiest to get them out again.”

“So a tenant was living there, not the owner himself?”

“That’s correct. He let the home out.”

“A problem tenant?” Stella clarified.

“They’re common.” Bronwyn nodded.

“Do you know what the problem was? Was it non-payment of the rent, or were there other issues?”

“Actually, I do know. I had a long heart-to-heart with the owner, and he told me everything. He originally rented this tenant the place because he thought he would be a good choice—he was a single, twenty-seven-year-old professional. But he quickly found out that the guy had taken on a different job which was only part time. He was home a lot of the day and he made a nuisance of himself in the neighborhood.”

“In what way?” Stella asked. This was sounding as if it might be critical to the case.

“He started borrowing things that he never gave back. He borrowed money. He asked for money. I believe from what the owner said that he used to get quite aggressive if the money wasn’t provided to him.” She shook her head sadly. “He must have had a problem. Drugs, alcohol, who knows. In these times, a lot of people aren’t right. It’s very sad, but it also does create a lot of stress in a situation like this.”

“Anything else?” Stella asked.

“Yes. He started looking into the homes, peering in when people were not home and sometimes when they were. Like a Peeping Tom. I remember my client said that neighbors called the police a couple of times to get him removed. They felt very uneasy, as they thought he seemed to be casing the homes. With all of this, the owner received numerous complaints about him from people in the area.”

"What happened? How did this play out?"

"The homeowner evicted him on the first of November, and then we immediately had the place deep cleaned and put it on show. It sold very fast. Within just a couple of weeks we had a lovely family take ownership. And there's never been a problem since."

She smiled at Stella.

Then she checked her screen again.

"No, it looks like the next closest matches would be a few months further back than that. In June, we sold a property about a mile away, and in May we made two sales, also within that suburb, but not close by."

"I think the first one sounds as if it could be important," Stella said. "Could you give me the homeowner's name and number? I'd like to find out more about his problem tenant, and if he has any idea where he moved to."

This was the very first indication she'd had of someone problematic in the neighborhood. Nobody had mentioned it because it had been a couple of months since the tenant had moved. People's memories were short once trouble had gone away. But there was a chance that this tenant had not just left on bad terms, but had planned to get payback.

The Taylors might even have been the ones who called the police on him, Stella theorized. That would have provided a motive, as the tenant could have blamed them for his eviction.

"Here you go." The real estate agent jotted the number down on one of her business cards and slid the card across to Stella. "I hope this helps you. I hope this helps all of us," she said, with sudden anxiety showing in her warm brown eyes.

Stella took the card and thanked Bronwyn again. Then she headed out of the coffee shop immediately and climbed back in her car.

There was no time like the present, and she wanted to get a feeling for where this house had been in relation to the Taylors.

She headed straight back down the road and turned into Partridge Street. As she drove the short distance, she realized that Bronwyn was right. There were a few For Sale signs already displayed along the way. Definitely more than the average should be, Stella realized. There was going to be a mass exodus, but even if buyers didn't read the news articles and join the dots for themselves, they would still want to know the reasons for the homes being on the market. That definitely made a sale more difficult.

There was number eight, on the corner. It was a gracious, two-story home that currently looked well cared for. She parked on the sidewalk, climbed out, and viewed the home from the front. Then she headed down to the crossroad to get another vantage point.

Scanning the house from these different angles, Stella realized that the large back windows in this home's upstairs section would have had a direct view of the Taylors' backyard and the rear section of their house.

So this neighbor could have scoped the home out through the windows and would have known its basic layout. Furthermore, he was clearly an antisocial person.

Serial killers were people who flouted society's rules and gloried in torture. Stella knew from her research that some of these individuals kept their secret side very well hidden.

But other killers were more obvious about their antisocial behavior, and what Bronwyn had described this tenant to be was a definite warning sign.

Standing in the road, she called the landlord's number that Bronwyn had given her, hoping that she'd get the information she needed fast, because she now felt impatient about following this new lead.

A man answered within two rings.

"Ed speaking," he said.

"This is Agent Fall, FBI," Stella introduced herself. "Bronwyn Hughes, the real estate agent who recently sold your house, gave me your number."

"She did?" Ed sounded puzzled. "Why's Bron giving my number out to the FBI? What's the issue here?"

"There was a murder two houses down. We're following up on leads and wanted to find out more about the tenant who lived in your place before you sold."

"A murder?" Ed's voice sharpened. "How horrific. I hadn't heard of it, but I'm vacationing in Hawaii at the moment. I must say, if that deadbeat was involved in a murder, I hope he pays for it. What a troublemaker!" His voice sharpened.

"Do you have a contact number for him? Or a forwarding address?" Stella asked.

"I sure do. And that's because I wanted to press charges and sue him for the outstanding rent. I wasn't successful but at least it means I know where he went. Otherwise, I'm sure he would have fled like a—like a rat!"

Ed sounded furious.

"Please give it to me," Stella said.

"Hope it's still in service. He's one of those guys who leaves such a trail of debt and disaster behind him that he might have changed his number or moved on. But here it is. He moved to Green Hills, which is close to Hartford, I think."

He read the details out to Stella and she keyed them into her phone.

"His name is Jay Bridges. I hope you find and prosecute him. I wasn't able to get my money, but he deserves to face the consequences of his behavior," Ed said darkly.

Stella felt renewed hope that this new suspect had such a poor track record. Now, the urgent job would be to trace him and for this, she needed help.

She called Maxwell.

He picked up after the first ring.

"Are you okay? Any news?" he asked quickly.

"I have news. I've found a new suspect who used to live close to the Taylors. He moved to Green Hills, but he was a troublemaker."

"In what way?"

"He was abusive, a Peeping Tom, and a compulsive borrower. Neighbors called the police out to him a few times. Two months ago, he got evicted."

Maxwell sounded eager to have a new direction to follow.

"Let's go and see him now," he said.

CHAPTER TWENTY TWO

With Maxwell driving and Stella navigating, they left the New Haven head office and turned onto the main road. Stella had no idea whether the given address for Jay Bridges would still be current, but it was at least a starting point.

"A problem tenant. With real problems?" Maxwell said. "Why weren't we told about this? Why did the immediate neighbors not mention it?"

"He moved away a couple of months ago so he wouldn't have been top of mind. You know how it is."

"Yes. People forget quickly. They might not even have thought it was relevant. Perhaps other neighbors didn't know, or see, what interactions Jay Bridges had with the Taylors. Then they wouldn't have realized," Maxwell said.

"There might have been some he targeted more than others. Definitely, he would have perceived the Taylors as wealthy."

"Yes. He could well have."

"People like that, career focused, might not have responded well to that kind of an individual. He might have pushed all the wrong buttons," Stella theorized.

"I hope we can find him and that he's still at his given address. Just let us locate him today. It can't be too much to ask?" Maxwell briefly took his hands off the wheel and raised them in a pleading gesture.

Stella couldn't help feeling a sense of futility when she thought about the size of Connecticut. Never mind that, the size of North America. Law enforcement felt like a spider web. It traversed the whole continent but there were gaps, and a tiny fly—aka a clever criminal—might be able to slip through those gaps and avoid the net.

Probably not forever, though it was not outside the bounds of possibility.

But what if Jay Bridges was able to successfully evade them long enough for this case to go cold?

Stella felt extremely stressed. A cold case involving a serial? That was absolutely not what society needed and it was not what she needed in her young career.

The miles could not pass by fast enough for her.

*

Jay had definitely downgraded his accommodations. Green Hills, the town they drove into forty-five minutes later, was distinctly less upmarket than the home he'd been kicked out of in Bridgeport. This neighborhood was packed full of smaller properties, shoulder to shoulder with each other.

Stella liked it. She thought it gave a neighborhood a friendly feel to have neighbors close by instead of hundreds of yards away, but she had to admit her views were probably shaped by the loneliness of growing up on a hardscrabble rural farm with nobody else for miles.

"This is the place." Maxwell pulled up and they stared at Jay's new given address.

It was a small one-story house. Modest and basic. It had a postage stamp–sized front yard. The grass was long and straggly. That was the first thing Stella noticed. Perhaps this was a hint that he might be actually in residence. He hadn't sounded like the type of person to care for his surroundings.

They parked outside, jumped out, and hustled to the front door. Maxwell knocked firmly.

Stella held her breath. She waited.

No answer. Nobody was coming to the door.

"Does he still live here?" Maxwell asked, frustrated.

Deciding to observe what she could, Stella set off around the house in a left-handed direction, scanning the windows as she went. The curtains were closed in the first, but the second was home to a couple of moving boxes, and a few piles of old tools, broken appliances, and other items that could well have just been dumped in the tiny spare room after a hasty move.

"There's definitely someone living here," she said, returning to the front door.

"There are tire tracks leading in and out of the garage. So yes, someone is here, but not home," Maxwell agreed.

"We need to locate his work. The real estate agent mentioned that he worked part time. But probably the landlord would have more details."

Feeling pressured, Stella called him again.

"I have one more question," she said as soon as he picked up. "The workplace. Do you know where Jay said he worked part time?"

"The electricity department in East Haven," he said. "Apparently he was a data capturer and fault logger who worked shifts."

"Thanks."

Stella disconnected.

This wasn't sounding good, because the electricity department was back in East Haven. Why had he moved all the way to Green Hills if his work was still there?

"Let's call them and find out more," she said, scrolling through her phone.

After a few seconds of hasty online searching, she had the number she needed. Standing right there on the doorstep of this humble and neglected home, she made the call.

"FBI Agent Fall calling, needing urgent information on a Mr. Jay Bridges. Does he work for your company? Is he at work at this time?" she asked.

"Hold on."

She was transferred immediately to a woman who answered, "HR office."

Stella repeated her question. "Agent Fall from the FBI, calling to find out more about a Mr. Jay Bridges."

"Hold on, please, ma'am."

Stella was immediately put on hold. Music blared from the receiver. She held her phone away from her ear to dampen its jangling assault.

Luckily, it took only a minute before the efficient woman was back.

"He doesn't work for us anymore, ma'am. His employment ended two months ago. Before that, he did work on a part-time shift basis, filling in when we had staff away."

Stella decided more information was needed.

"Can you explain why his employment ended?"

"Um—" The woman hesitated.

"We are busy with a murder investigation," Stella said. "We can subpoena you to appear in court and provide the information. However it would be much easier, and help us hugely, if you could just say."

"All right." With this threat as the alternative, the woman sounded relieved to comply. "There were a couple of reasons why we terminated Mr. Bridges' employment. Firstly, he was unreliable and consistently clocked in late, and missed a couple of shifts without notice."

"Go on?" Stella said.

"Secondly, we received complaints from a few colleagues that he was interfering with them. He was asking them for money, borrowing things, becoming aggressive if they refused. He was accused of being a stalker. We decided in view of these two separate issues to terminate his employment."

"Thank you," Stella said.

She put down the phone and turned to Maxwell.

"He was fired," she said.

Maxwell frowned. "Fired, and he's living here, but not home. I think the quickest way might be to get an official track on his phone."

"Let's do it," Stella said.

Maxwell called the FBI New Haven offices immediately to set up the track. While he spoke to the techs, they both retreated back to the shelter of the car. It was a cold, bleak winter day and the wind was stinging.

Stella hoped they would be able to do the track. It often depended on the model of phone. She knew from experience that older phones didn't have sophisticated tracking in them and could only go by GPS triangulation, which was not accurate. New phones had technology in place so sophisticated that a user could be pinpointed to within a few yards.

That was, of course, assuming the user had not disabled the phone's functionality. There were ways to do that. The most efficient of those being turning it off.

She felt anxious as Maxwell continued with the back and forth to the technical department. However, she personally felt sure that a guy like this would have a newer phone. If he was a hustler who begged and borrowed and threatened, he'd need all the latest communication technology to harass his targets.

"Okay." Maxwell disconnected, sounding pleased. "They've found the signal. They're going to track it from the headquarters and will then radio directions through to us. They said he doesn't have a vehicle registered in his name at this time. So he must be in something rented, loaned, or stolen."

A moment later, the radio crackled into life. Maxwell started the car and reversed at top speed, swinging onto the road.

"The suspect must be in a vehicle. He is heading along Interstate 91 in a northerly direction," the technician said.

Northerly? Stella felt confused. Where was he going on the interstate?

"We're joining up with the interstate in a few minutes. Do you see my vehicle?" he asked.

Crackling silence followed for a few beats.

"Yes. I've picked up your vehicle, sir," the technician said. "You are approximately twenty miles behind the suspect."

"I'm going to shorten that distance," Maxwell said, sounding resolute. "Hold on tight, and control, keep me in the loop."

Stella was pressed back in her seat as Maxwell turned on the unmarked's lights and siren and flattened his foot.

CHAPTER TWENTY THREE

The car leaped forward and in a few moments, Stella and Maxwell were speeding in the fast lane. Stella could see the focused tension in every fiber of Maxwell's body. His hands were clamped to the wheel. His eyes were glued to the road ahead, apart from regular lightning glances into his mirrors to check the space around him.

"I'll send out an advisory to traffic police in the areas ahead. They might be able to assist," the technician said, his voice crackling over the radio. "At the moment your suspect is still on the interstate and still heading north. There are exits every couple of miles and I'll advise you immediately if he changes course."

"That'll be great." Maxwell sounded casual but Stella knew he felt as keyed up as she did.

Stella was consumed with impatience about catching up those precious twenty miles, which represented a totally new direction in the investigation. She felt glad Maxwell was at the wheel. His driving was slick, speedy, and smoothly coordinated, as if he was one with the car.

They were flying along the highway, going at a speed where the road was telescoping in front of her and cars ahead were ducking out of the way as quick as they could. And yet, although Stella felt filled with adrenaline and as if she was ten times more alive and alert than usual, she didn't feel afraid.

She guessed that showed how much she trusted Maxwell. It was more than just his driving ability, Stella decided. She trusted him as a person. That said a lot for his character, and as she acknowledged this, she felt a sense of peace.

For a while she had been doubtful and mistrustful of him and it felt as if her world had broken apart. Now, she felt she was coming back to the truth.

And to reality, she thought, catching her breath as he braked sharply.

"Sorry," he muttered, without looking at her, not daring to take his focus from the road as they reached a slower-moving knot of cars.

"How are we doing?" Stella asked the tech on the other side.

"Fifteen-mile gap. You're catching up fast."

"Not as fast as we should be," Maxwell said. "That guy must also be flooring it. I wonder why. Perhaps he's doing a runner out of state."

Stella thought the timing would make sense if Jay Bridges had recently found out that the crimes had hit the news. Knowing the heat was on might make a man decide to flee. Especially if he was guilty from the get-go.

"I can't go faster," Maxwell said, acknowledging the vehicle's capabilities and the safety margins he needed to maintain.

"You'll catch him. You've already narrowed the gap," the tech reassured him.

"There's still too much space ahead. If he's running, he's panicking. But once he stops panicking, he's going to remember to turn his phone off," Maxwell said.

Stella caught her breath at this unwanted possibility.

"Signal's still there," the tech stated calmly.

"Hopefully he's going too fast to think about it," she said, but she couldn't help feeling cold inside. A moment's logical thought, a press of a button, a swerve off the highway, and their suspect who was so clearly pinpointed might disappear.

"Tell me when there's a four-mile gap," Maxwell said. "I'm going to turn off my siren. That noise is audible from a long way back. I don't want him to get warning, and to try and evade us because he senses we're following him."

"Great idea," Stella praised. She thought approaching the last few miles in stealth would give them a decided advantage.

"Will do. He's still on the interstate. Still going north. Approaching the Massachusetts state line. Signal is stable," the tech said.

As the gray tarmac and the wintry landscape flashed by, Stella knew that slowly, this gap was reducing. Although her attention was focused on the highway, keeping a lookout for any traffic that Maxwell might suddenly need to avoid, she was also aware of the landscape passing by. They were leaving the urban boundary behind and heading out into the countryside.

Did he have a hideout here? He didn't seem like a guy to plan too far ahead, Stella thought hopefully. But he must have a destination in mind.

If this guy was smart, Stella thought, he'd wait until he neared the next big town or city and then cut his phone, and then lose himself in slow-moving traffic.

She hoped he wasn't that smart.

"Get out of my way!" Impatiently, Maxwell blasted his horn at a truck driver passing a slower eighteen-wheeler. The horn was barely audible over the siren, but Stella guessed it made him feel better.

"Damned trucks!" Maxwell complained. "Can't they have any patience?"

Stella did not miss the irony of his words, but being around so many other cars was making her realize all over again how risky this chase was.

As soon as the truck driver was back in his lane, Maxwell flattened his foot again, but had to swerve almost immediately as an impatient BMW driver veered into the fast lane.

The guy didn't back down, but instead shook his fist self-righteously at the passing agents.

"Special people," Stella said. She felt wound up with tension inside but tried her best to make light of the near-collision.

"You're approximately four miles behind the suspect," the radio tech advised.

"Okay." Maxwell turned off the lights and siren. The silence felt deafening. Stella knew this headlong journey was now even riskier without the warning signals in place. Maxwell slowed down slightly. Going any faster would be too dangerous. Stella's stomach was knotted. In just a minute or two, they would finally catch up. Would they reach him? What car was he driving?

In silence, they sped along. With traffic heavier Maxwell was taking more risks, since he couldn't use the siren to push other traffic out of the way. Now, he was zigzagging in between the cars, which took hair's-breadth judgment.

"Two miles," the radio tech calmly informed them.

They whooshed past other traffic as he veered into the right lane, swung the unmarked between two vans, and then came out of a blind swerve that made Stella catch her breath, swinging back into the left lane again.

"Surely we must have nearly caught up by now?" Stella felt worried.

Had Jay decided at the last minute to make himself invisible?

"One mile," the tech told them.

Stella leaned forward, wishing they knew more. Now that they were past the next town's main exit ramp, traffic was heavier. There were so many cars on the road. High-speed chases like this were dangerous in traffic. If he panicked and ran, there was a chance someone would crash.

"You're a quarter-mile away from him," the tech said.

Stella realized she'd been holding her breath. She let it out and breathed in deeply.

"According to my satnav, you're now two hundred yards from him. Can you see him?" the tech asked.

"Traffic's heavy," Maxwell replied. "But if he's in the bunch of cars ahead, maybe now would be a good time to scare him."

He switched on the lights and siren again.

"One hundred yards."

They were almost on him. Where would he be?

Stella guessed since he'd been speeding, he'd be in the fast lane. There were three cars closely grouped ahead in that lane. All were sedans. One silver, one white, one red.

As Stella watched, the red one—in the middle of the group—veered suddenly right and darted the other side of a truck.

"That's him!" she said. "It must be!"

"Agreed," Maxwell said. "Let's chase him down."

This was nail biting. Had they made the correct call?

"He's taking the next exit," Stella said.

"You're twenty yards away," the tech said. "Do you have an ID on the car?"

"Red Ford. Driver's panicking," Maxwell observed, as the red car darted in between two other vehicles. Horns blared.

"Looks like your target is taking the exit," the tech said.

"Yup," Maxwell said. "That's him then. We're also taking this exit. Any police cars in the neighborhood? We could use some help. We need to get this guy before he causes an accident."

"I'm radioing for support. We actually had backup in place, further along the highway. They'll have to come back this way now," the tech said.

"Just us, then," Maxwell acknowledged.

He sped along. The driver of the red car was seriously panicking. He flew through a red light without even braking and Stella clapped her hand over her mouth as he barely missed a collision.

With the siren blaring, Maxwell braked only a moment before rocketing through the same intersection. Jay was now veering back and forth across the double-lane road. Maxwell kept on his tail. Stella was sure that if this driver got the chance he would swing right into a crossroad and try to lose them again.

And he did. He braked so suddenly he left thick black tracks on the road. Stella grabbed the dashboard as Maxwell hit the brakes, swearing under his breath as the guy veered desperately down a side road.

Brakes shrieked from behind them and a cacophony of horns erupted.

"We're not going to make it," Stella said, watching the grille of the truck behind get bigger and bigger in the back mirror.

"We will." Wrenching the wheel, Maxwell slewed the car to the right and followed. With a bellow of its horn and a scream of brakes, the truck veered past them.

"You're on Plantation Drive. There's a police car that might just be able to make it up ahead," the tech said.

"Please," Maxwell said. "This guy's going to cause a crash otherwise. And soon."

"We've got your backup in place. Roadblock ahead." The tech's words filled Stella with relief.

The red car sped around the corner ahead, saw the roadblock, and then hit the brakes so hard he really did slide. It was nerve-wrenching to watch as the car sailed sideways, tires screaming, missing an oncoming SUV by mere inches.

But there was nowhere he could go. A police car swerved into the other lane, blocking the turn in front of him, lights flashing. Maxwell veered sideways, getting behind the red car so he couldn't try and flee back the way he'd come.

They'd cornered him.

And even better, they'd managed not to cause a crash in the process.

With a scream of brakes, the red car stopped.

Maxwell squealed the unmarked to a stop behind him.

As soon as Jay was effectively bracketed, Stella jumped out of the car and drew her gun. A cornered suspect was highly likely to shoot.

But it seemed Jay didn't have a gun on him. The red car's door opened slowly. Peering inside, Stella thought the driver looked shocked as the police and agents surrounded him. He climbed out, staring from one of them to the other.

"Jay Bridges?" Maxwell asked.

"That's me."

"You're under arrest."

“What is this?” he asked innocently. “I’ve done nothing wrong. What is happening here? You guys need to let me go. I have rights!”

Looking at him, Stella could see exactly how he’d managed to fool the landlord. He was a preppy-looking guy, with his short, brown, wavy hair and even features. The kind of guy you might trust enough to loan money to—the first time, anyway. It was only after a closer look that you noticed his shifty eyes and restless limbs, Stella thought.

“We’re not talking here,” Maxwell said. Turning to the patrol officer, he said, “Let’s bring him in to the closest police precinct and question him there. Charges so far include reckless driving and failing to obey an officer of the law. We will hopefully be able to add to that list soon.”

CHAPTER TWENTY FOUR

Fifteen minutes later, Stella and Maxwell were ready to question Jay. Local police had swarmed in to help, and he had been arrested and brought into the closest police precinct. After their headlong chase, Stella hadn't had a clue which one it was, but it proved to be the Chicopee Police Department in Massachusetts.

It was a small, attractive police station that was typically suburban, set among an area of trim, neat houses. There were a few locals waiting inside, and all of them turned and stared in astonishment as the handcuffed suspect was hustled through to the interview room. Serious crime in this area was clearly not high. This was an unusual sight that would be talked about.

"Shall we interview him together?" Maxwell asked Stella.

She nodded. "Yes. Let's both go in."

They walked to the interview room door. Outside, Stella paused for a moment to gather her thoughts. They could not afford to make a mistake in this questioning. This might be their only chance to pin down a killer who had evaded them up till now.

Jay looked up as soon as the door opened. He clocked their arrival with a narrow-eyed gaze.

"I've done nothing wrong," he protested immediately.

"Why did you run as soon as I turned on the siren?" Maxwell asked.

"I didn't. I was just trying to get where I was going."

"Why were you in such a hurry, then?"

"That's how I always drive, man," he protested, trying for defensive innocence.

Maxwell shook his head.

"We have dashcam footage. No reasonable person would believe your version. You recklessly tried to evade us. You drove dangerously and could easily have caused an accident. So let's get down to the reasons why."

He scooted into a seat opposite the suspect and Stella sat next to him. She was happy for Maxwell to ask most of the questions. He would pressure Jay, tough and aggressive, leaving her to read his responses.

"Firstly, whose car is this? You don't have a vehicle in your name."

"It's—it's a friend's car. He's loaning it to me for a while."

"Which friend?"

"Guy named Byron." Jay mumbled the answer, clearly not pleased with the question.

"We'll see about that," Maxwell said calmly.

Jay shifted in his chair. He glanced at the door. It didn't take much skill in body language to know that he was not comfortable with being here. Not at all.

"A few months ago, you rented a home in Bridgeport," Stella said.

Jay's eyes widened. He quickly arranged his features into an innocent expression, but Stella hadn't missed that moment. Jay knew exactly why he was sitting in this interview room.

"When I say 'rented,' that's probably not the best word. Your behavior caused you to get evicted."

"It wasn't like that!" Jay protested. "The owner wanted to sell!"

"The owner wanted you out. You made trouble with the neighbors. Looking into their houses, casing them out. Borrowing money. Causing trouble."

Jay shrugged defensively. "So I hit tough times. So I was looking for a bit of help. That isn't a crime."

"Murder is a crime. You must know what happened to the Taylors."

Jay regarded them through those shifty-looking eyes.

"I knew you were going to come looking for me," he said. "I didn't do it. But I knew you'd think I did. Someone from my old workplace called me this morning. They told me what happened. I knew you might want to pick on somebody innocent, so I was going to spend a week or two with a friend of mine, out of state."

As far as excuses went, Stella thought this sounded weak. Jay was not convincing her with his story so far. But once they'd finished dissecting his flimsy reasons for running, then scrutinizing his alibi would take this further.

"Why would you have bothered to endanger yourself and everyone else if you were innocent?" Maxwell insisted.

"Why would I want to be dragged into a police station and accused of a crime I didn't commit?" Jay retorted.

"You knew the Taylors?" Stella asked.

“The Taylors? Not so well. I might have spoken to them once or twice.”

His gaze slipped away. This man was evasive and shifty as hell, Stella saw. She didn’t trust a word he said.

“Did you ever borrow money from them? Or try to?” Maxwell continued the questioning.

Jay shrugged. “Like I said, I was in a difficult situation. I asked a few people for help. I might have asked them. I don’t remember.”

Taking refuge in generalizations would not get him far, Stella decided. It was time to cut straight to the chase and confirm his alibi.

“Where were you on the night they were murdered?” she asked. “Did your ‘friend’ tell you which night it was?”

“He said it was the night before last,” Jay mumbled.

“Correct. So, your movements on Tuesday night?”

Jay shrugged. “What time would that be?”

“You give us your timeframe,” Maxwell demanded.

“I was at home.”

“Were you with anyone? Can anyone confirm you were at the Green Hills residence?”

“I was alone.”

“Did you go out at all?”

Jay shrugged again.

Stella was starting to feel suspicious about his evasiveness. But suspicion was not enough reason to accuse him. They needed facts, and Jay was clearly going to force them to get the facts the hard way, by gathering evidence on where he’d been and who he’d spoken to.

Maxwell frowned. “Show us your phone,” he said.

“My phone?” He looked startled.

“Yes. Your phone. It’s there in the plastic dish in front of you. Unlock it and hand it over to me.”

Jay looked thunderously angry.

“My phone is my private life!”

“Should have thought of that before endangering other people’s lives with reckless driving,” Maxwell said, folding his arms to make sure Jay understood his utter lack of sympathy.

Sullenly, Jay reached for his phone, unlocked it, and handed it over.

“Let’s have a look,” Maxwell said.

Stella knew he was going to carefully scan the calls and messages. She couldn’t wait to see if he noticed anything obvious.

Maxwell snorted. Stella saw a brief flicker of amusement in his eyes.

"For a start, I should tell you Byron wants his car back."

Jay pressed his lips together. He'd flushed deep red, Stella noted.

"He's been trying to get it back since Monday. Apparently you borrowed it to go to church on Sunday and never gave it back. Interesting," Maxwell noted. "Let's see what else we can find that might give us more information on you, Mr. Bridges, seeing you don't want to provide it yourself."

Maxwell scrolled through the phone.

"Okay." He sounded thoughtful. "Who's Kelly?"

"A neighbor," Jay said.

"A neighbor in Green Hills?"

"Yeah," Jay muttered. "She lives next door."

"Okay."

Maxwell continued his scrolling without saying anything further. Stella in the meantime observed Jay.

He was looking fidgety and uneasy. There was definitely a strong reason why he was holding back. But Stella didn't know what it was.

Abruptly, Maxwell stood up.

"Let's speak outside," he told Stella.

Still holding Jay's phone, he walked out, with Stella rushing behind him.

"I don't know what to make of this," he muttered. "He was harassing Kelly on the night of the crime. He sent four messages to her between six and seven p.m. asking for money to help him get to his old mother who had just broken her arm."

Stella blinked.

"Lies and more lies," she observed.

"Yeah. He just makes stuff up randomly. He also tried to harass someone else whose number isn't saved, saying, *'I see you're not home. Are you gonna be home soon, I need cash bro.'* That was at about eight. So definitely, for the early part of the evening, he was canvassing neighbors on this side. And he was walking around and looking into homes as it seems he likes to do."

Stella sighed. "It's not enough for an alibi."

"No," Maxwell agreed.

She looked at him. They both made identical faces.

"He could have done it. The timeline still allows for it."

"Yes," Maxwell said.

He didn't sound convinced, though, which mirrored Stella's feelings.

"I'm not arguing with the fact he had motive or opportunity. But I am battling with the impression I have of him, and his personality. He doesn't seem to be a pre-planner," she explained.

"I feel the same." Maxwell nodded.

"The killer was very disciplined. A careful planner. This guy is random. He just bounces from source to source hoping for one of the sources to open up."

"That is exactly my issue with him also. He's showing a different mindset from what I pictured. It's like Jay would never have had the capacity to do what the killer did."

"And yet, we can't release him. It would be wrong. He is a suspect, Maxwell. He was in the area. He interacted with the neighbors. There was a big history of misdoings and threats and broken promises."

"I know."

"But he's twenty-seven years old and apart from getting warned off by the police, he has no criminal record."

"Exactly."

Stella could see Maxwell was thinking exactly the way she was. This was not an easy situation.

This was a strong suspect. He had no clear alibi. He could easily have gone anywhere on his borrowed wheels. He'd tried to evade police.

Stella felt absolutely torn.

Circumstantially this could easily be their guy. But psychologically he didn't tick the boxes.

Stella acknowledged the main problem in their serious dilemma.

"If we go ahead with the charges, it means we might just be missing out on the real killer."

Maxwell sighed. "That's my thought, too. We cannot afford to miss the real killer. We can't. Whoever it is, is too dangerous. Also, as it stands, we don't have enough on this guy. We will need to do our homework big-time. We'll need to pull camera footage all along the route, track his car's plate, gather witness reports. It might turn up some evidence but that's going to take days."

"Let's hold him for now," Stella said. "Let's give it a few more hours and go back to that case and go through everything we have again. Knowing that if we do arrest the wrong guy, it's going to be nothing short of a catastrophe."

There was everything at stake here.

They turned and went into the police station's admin office, hoping they could find a spare corner to regroup and review what they had so far. Otherwise Stella feared they were heading into a lose-lose situation that would be the worst possible scenario.

CHAPTER TWENTY FIVE

Stella and Maxwell sat down in the Chicopee Police Department's admin office, using a desk which the sergeant had kindly cleared. The back office was a small, cluttered, busy place with a faint whiff of cigarette smoke blowing in through the back door, which was opened a crack. Outside, the smokers were huddled against the wall to shelter from the day's cold.

Over the months she had been with the FBI, Stella had learned to open her laptop and notebook and work absolutely anywhere, shutting out her surroundings. That was what she did now.

Within a minute, she wasn't aware of the scent of smoke, or the flickering light above her, or the laughter on the other side of the room as three uniformed cops shared a humorous moment. All she was focused on was the timeline, witnesses, and details of this case.

Was there any evidence, anywhere, that could point to someone other than this erratic and improbable suspect?

"I've received the cold case report," Maxwell said beside her. "Remember I requested it from the FBI office?"

"Good." Perhaps that might give them a new direction. They sure needed it now.

"I'll forward it to you, so you can also take a look. If both of us read through, it's double the chance of picking up on the finer details and similarities. My main problem is with the gap in time. I'm battling to get past that. There have been no other similar cases within the past ten years. Nothing has come up in that timeframe in the cold case records. But here you go."

He quickly tapped keys, and Stella waited a beat. The file arrived in her inbox and she focused all her attention on it.

The cold case had occurred long ago and she could see why Maxwell was immediately put off by that massive, ten-year gap. Scrutinizing the details definitely seemed like a last resort. But now, with all other options exhausted, they needed to give it more attention. This was the only case that had similarities with their current one. Both victims were husband and wife. Both were murdered in a bloody and violent way. And in both cases, an extremely valuable item had been taken from the home and then discarded.

If these same cases had been a month apart, Stella acknowledged, they would be assigning all available personnel to the investigation. This would become one of the FBI's major focus points nationally. Resources would be poured into it.

But it wasn't. The murders were a decade apart and they had taken place in different states—Connecticut and Delaware. With that time gap, Stella did think that logically it was more likely that someone had committed a copycat crime, or read about the cold case and decided it would be a good way to deflect attention from their real motive.

"Ten years ago, Jay would have been seventeen, and most likely too young to commit that crime himself, especially with no criminal record or juvenile delinquency report before or since," she said thoughtfully, her mind turning to their only suspect still in custody. "If he knew about that murder, then it would be more likely he copied it. But given his personality, I also have difficulty with the idea of him stealing and then discarding a valuable item."

"I do, too," Maxwell admitted.

She worried that Jay was not, in fact, their suspect, and that the real killer was still at large. So she decided she was going to do what she knew her father would have done. She was going to read through every word of the case. He wouldn't have let a detail escape that might link the two cases together in other ways. Nor would she.

Stella began reading.

She took in the circumstances of the crime, the background, the timeframe. There were many basic similarities but these were not unusual for the general circumstances of such a crime. Both crimes had been committed late at night, but Stella knew from her own university studies that serious crimes were more commonly committed at night. She recalled that the hours between eight and ten p.m. were prime time for violent crimes and this overlapped with the timeframe of both cases. Reading on, she noted that both sets of victims were well off and lived in a wealthy area. Again, that was not surprising, since both crimes involved a high-value item that had been stolen, though later recovered.

Stella noted with interest that one of the detectives in the cold case had drawn possible parallels between this case and an even older one, eight years previously. The cases had some similar characteristics, but the previous one had been in Ohio and had involved a victim living on his own.

Frustratingly, there seemed to be nothing more linking this cold case with their current one in any way. The detectives working on the Delaware case had arrested a vagrant on suspicion, but he'd been able to prove he was with others on the night of the crime. Their attention had also focused for a while on the wife's older brother. They'd had a conflicted relationship and he had a history of assault. However, he'd been living in a different state at the time and although he had no alibi for the night of the crime, as he'd been alone, the detectives had painstakingly calculated that it wouldn't have been possible in terms of timing for him to have clocked out of work, traveled there, and committed the crime. So he'd been cleared, too.

The detectives had reported that neighbors had not seen or heard anything and apart from the random presence of the vagrant, there had been no problems or issues in the area.

Stella paged through the photographs. There were several of the house, taken from many angles. It was a sleek, modern, double-story residence. It had a pretty road name. Thirty-five Mockingbird Avenue. Staring at it, Stella realized it looked like a showpiece home, just as the Taylors' did. That made her think about another possible similarity, which she quickly checked.

Sure enough, the Delaware victims also had no children, although they had been older, in their mid-forties.

No children was interesting, and definitely unusual, but it didn't get her anywhere and could also be logically explained. No children pointed to a career-focused couple, with possibly more disposable income, which in turn meant a slightly bigger chance of valuables within the home attracting unwanted attention. She couldn't deduce more from it.

Career-wise, the husband had worked as a computer programmer, and the wife had been an account manager for an investment bank. So there were no workplace links between them and the Taylors.

Opening her browser, a quick internet check showed her that the Delaware case had also created a media stir, both at the time, and then again—a much smaller ripple—when the missing vase had been found. As she skimmed a few of the old reports, she saw that the news articles were varied, in terms of the levels of panic they generated, and also their accuracy. Wild theories had been proposed by some of the journalists, but with no progress made on the case, the news reports had dried up in a surprisingly short time.

"I'm trying as hard as I can here but I'm not finding what we need," she said.

"Nothing concrete enough?" Maxwell asked.

"Well, there are parallels, but there aren't. They are very similar types of crime and the victims fit a similar profile. But apart from that, there is nothing linking them."

"Could this case have been written up somewhere, and someone found out about it and decided to copy it?"

"That's what I'm thinking, too," Stella said. "It did make waves at the time. I looked it up online and there were media reports about it. Someone could have remembered the details and decided to copy the MO."

"So we're back to Jay Bridges as a copycat." Maxwell sounded resigned.

"Yes, we are," she acknowledged.

"Not where we want to be."

That reality hit her with a thud.

"No. It isn't where we want to be. But maybe we should now play the cards we've been dealt," she suggested.

"You mean?"

"I mean, we should try and piece together the evidence on him that might be there, and we've missed. Maybe he threatened the Taylors," Stella said.

"You think?" Maxwell still didn't seem convinced.

Stella shrugged. "He might be more intelligent than we are giving him credit for. Perhaps he's intelligent enough to act like someone who isn't."

Maxwell raised a hand to his forehead and rubbed his temples. Stella watched sympathetically. This case was giving her a headache too.

"I just don't understand why a guy like that, who seems to be so short of cash and such a chancer, would take a valuable item from the home and then abandon it."

Stella leaned back against the wall, stretching her shoulders. Like Maxwell, she realized she was holding a lot of tension inside.

"I know. It doesn't fit his personality. The only reason I can think of is that some psychopathic killers have the side they show to the world, and then they have a hidden side. If Jay's side he shows to the world is the creepy guy who's always borrowing and asking and casing out places, that's what it is. It is unusual but it's not impossible. It doesn't mean he couldn't have a hidden side which might be very different and deadly."

"Which he unleashes every so often?"

"Exactly. And which could be invisible until he chooses to show it."

Maxwell nodded. "Okay. So basically, when that side comes out, then all bets are off?"

"Yes."

"How would we know if he was that kind of a person?"

That was a good question, Stella thought. Apart from the murder itself, what other clues might there be?

"You think the neighbors would know?" Maxwell asked.

"Yes, and I think the Taylors' housekeeper would know. If this guy came around during the day begging and threatening, she might have had more interaction with him. Or they could have warned her about him."

"The housekeeper!" Maxwell snapped his fingers. "I got hold of Maria earlier today. She didn't want to talk to me, as she was at her son's high school music recital, so I cut her some slack on that. But she gave me her address and said we should call her later in the day and she'd be available."

"Okay. We have a starting point," Stella said.

"You go and interview Maria," Maxwell decided. "I think you'd have the ability to get her to open up much faster than I do. Depending on what she says, we can decide where to go next, and in the meantime, I'll continue working on Jay Bridges. I can ask him if he knew about the Delaware crime, or if he ever lived in that state."

Stella felt pleased that they had a concrete plan of action lined up. And she looked forward to speaking to Maria. This was another witness who had slipped through the cracks so far, and needed to be followed up.

Stella took the number Maxwell had given her and called the housekeeper immediately.

"Maria speaking," a calm voice answered.

"Maria, this is Agent Fall from the FBI."

There was a pause. She felt Maria was preparing herself for what was to come.

"This is to get information about my employer, Mrs. Taylor?" Maria asked.

"That's correct. We're investigating the murder and we have some questions. Would it be possible for us to meet face to face?" Stella asked.

"Sure. I can meet you. I live in downtown New Haven. Do you want to meet me at my house?"

"If you're happy with that, it'll be great," Stella said. Calculating how long the drive back would take at normal speed, she said, "I can be there in just over an hour."

"I'll send you the address," Maria said.

Stella headed out, hoping that between her and Maxwell, one of them would get somewhere in the next few hours. If Jay Bridges had threatened the Taylors, or had particular issues with them, she felt sure Maria would know.

*

After getting caught up in traffic that caused a frustrating delay, Stella finally walked up the stairs of the three-story apartment building where Maria lived. The building wasn't far from Stella's own.

She tapped on the front door, and when it opened, she came face to face with a petite, round-faced woman with a cloud of dark hair. Maria looked about forty years old, and was only about five feet tall. She exuded an air of worry.

"Agent Fall," Stella introduced herself politely. She stepped into the small apartment. It was colorfully decorated with brightly upholstered furniture, patterned rugs, and a variety of paintings, and she wasn't surprised that it was as neat as a pin.

Maria walked into the tiny living. Stella sat down on a floral armchair. Maria took the blue sofa opposite.

"I hope I am not in trouble," Maria said immediately. "I was so shocked when I heard what had happened, and afraid as well. I could not take in that I arrived for work and there had been a terrible crime and both the Taylors were dead."

"Unfortunately that's what happened, ma'am," Stella agreed.

"I felt sick. I was dizzy. I actually had to sit down on the sidewalk as I thought I was going to faint or throw up. One of the security guards there said I should go home. He gave me a ride back to the bus stop and I went home. I thought of calling the Taylors but—they were both gone. I still don't know what to do. I know I need to go back to the agency and apply for a new job but I don't feel ready," Maria confessed.

Stella was glad to have more of an explanation of why she'd left the scene.

"I think a couple of weeks' vacation would do you good. It's very traumatic to have to process something like this," she sympathized.

"So, why are you here?" Maria asked tentatively. "How can I help?"

Stella decided to ask some open-ended questions to begin.

"How long have you known the Taylors?"

"I was employed by them three years ago. So ever since then."

"Did you work for them full time?"

"I worked for them five days a week. The workdays were flexible," Maria explained. "They worked very hard during the week and often weren't home, so I would sometimes skip a day and work weekends, especially if they had visitors on the weekend."

"Who visited them?" Stella asked.

"They occasionally had work friends over for dinner. Neighbors. Sometimes family, when they were in town, but that wasn't often. They didn't throw big parties."

"Did you notice if there were any problems with any of the people they socialized with?"

Maria shook her head thoughtfully. "No, not at all. I never saw a problem with anyone. They were quiet, friendly people. They treated everyone well. Mrs. Taylor never raised her voice."

It was time to get into the specifics.

"Did you ever speak to a neighbor from two houses down? Mr. Jay Bridges? This is what he looks like." Stella showed her a photo.

Maria inspected it carefully.

"I saw him in the neighborhood, yes. He used to go from house to house asking for money. I would often notice him walking around the area. He used to greet me, and was quite friendly to me, but I know he got into fights with other people. I remember there was shouting a few times at the nearby homes, and somebody called the police once."

This added to the evidence of fights and threats. It was forming a picture.

"Did he ever ask you for money?" Stella said.

"No," Maria said.

Stella guessed that as a seasoned con artist, Jay would have known to focus on the bigger targets—the homeowners. People with money and cars. Maria hadn't been on his radar at all. But knowing he could behave so differently with different people, and turn on the threats when he needed to, was a red flag.

"Did the Taylors ever complain about Mr. Bridges?"

"No. Not at all. Not to me, anyway. But they did not speak badly of anyone to me. I did not share in their private lives," Maria said. "Once or twice, as I left, I did see him heading in the direction of the home. So he might have knocked on their door after I had gone."

That was interesting, Stella thought. Had Jay deliberately waited until the housekeeper wasn't there to guard the gates?

"Were there any other service providers or delivery people who came to the house in the past few weeks? Anyone who had issues with the Taylors, or showed too much of an interest in the home's contents?" Stella tried.

"No. They got regular grocery deliveries but I collected those at the door. They had a landscaper who worked once a week, and in summer they had a company who looked after the pool. I think they might have had gas bottles replaced a couple of weeks ago, but they have used the same firm for that ever since I've worked there. There was nobody new in the home recently, and nobody who gave me a bad feeling."

"Thank you. That's all I need," Stella said.

She turned and left Maria's tidy apartment, feeling thoughtful. There had been a good chance that Jay had interacted with the Taylors if he had canvassed the neighborhood, but the information she needed was still tantalizingly beyond her reach.

Stella decided to go back to the neighbors themselves and ask more about Jay's behavior.

She climbed into her car and headed to Bridgeport, hoping that this time she would be able to learn exactly what Jay had been getting up to, what he'd said, and who he had threatened.

CHAPTER TWENTY SIX

Arriving at Parkway Drive, Stella's first stop was the Parsons' home. Seeing a car in their driveway, she decided to go straight there. She parked on the side of the road, planning what questions she would ask.

But, as she got out of her car, she heard a friendly "Hello!" from across the street.

Graham Haddow had his front door open and was looking out curiously at her.

"Agent Fall? You're here again?" he called.

"Yes. I'm checking some more facts. I need to speak to you as well. Do you have a moment?" Stella asked, thinking that he might have been heading out.

"I was going out. But that can wait," Graham said, opening the door wider.

If Graham was going out to the store, she should talk to him first, Stella decided. She jogged across the road and walked inside.

"I'm heading into town to organize a moving company. It's time, I'm afraid," Graham said, looking sad.

Walking into the cozy home, Stella could see he'd already made headway with the process of packing up. Looking at the large cardboard box in the hall, and the empty hall table free from its ornaments and memorabilia, made her feel strangely sad. It was evidence of the aftershocks that disrupted people's lives following a crime like this.

"Can we sit down for a moment?" she asked.

"Of course we can. Please, come through to the living room."

Now that she was actually inside, Stella thought he looked faintly stressed, as if yet another visit from the FBI was too much for him to handle right now. She remembered last time she'd been inside the home, when he'd been welcoming and had offered her cookies. Now, he was clearly in the throes of packing, and in a different mindset. She got the impression he had already moved on. That he was no longer deeply involved in this community.

She followed him through to the living room. It looked very different from the last time. It, too, was filled with boxes containing ornaments, books, crockery, and linens. Last time she remembered it as being tidy and welcoming, if a bit shabby. Now it seemed disordered, as if its identity was being stripped away. Most of the chairs had been moved to the corner. Only two dining room chairs were available for seating. Graham sat down on one and Stella perched on the other.

"Mr. Haddow, I wanted to ask you about a neighbor who moved away a couple of months ago. He lived down the cross street and was a tenant in the home. His name was Jay Bridges."

Stella hoped the name might ring a bell. However, it didn't seem to have any immediate significance for Graham.

"Jay Bridges?" he asked, frowning.

"I'll show you a photo," Stella said.

She opened her phone and scrolled through. Then she stood up and walked over to him, to show him the picture.

As soon as Graham saw it, his face lit up.

"Ah, of course. Him! You know, I don't think I ever knew his name. I just knew him as that very entitled young man who came around wanting to borrow things. I'm afraid I was rather short-tempered with him."

Stella smiled. She could not believe Graham being short-tempered. Jay must have pushed his boundaries to their limits.

"Do you remember if there was any bad blood between him and the Taylors?" Stella asked.

Graham nodded thoughtfully.

"You know, now you mention it, there were a couple of incidents that upset them. I remember Diane speaking about it after he left."

Stella sat straighter.

"Can you tell me more about what she said?"

Suddenly, there was light at the end of a very long and dark tunnel. If Graham could add the missing pieces, then they might finally get a clear picture of what had caused this brutal crime.

"Let me think," he said, frowning.

At that moment, from the kitchen, his phone rang.

"Excuse me," he said, scrambling up. "That will be the real estate agent, wanting to confirm a few details. They already have a potential buyer lined up but haven't yet had the chance to come here and take photos. I've been back and forth with them since this morning."

With a stressed sigh, he hurried to the kitchen.

"Hello?" Stella heard him say. "Can I call you back?"

He paused. "You're sitting with the client? Alright, if we're quick. You need to confirm what? The patterns on the cornices? And the color of the carpet in the upstairs rooms?" Graham sounded incredulous.

He paused again.

"And the type of light fittings?" He sighed. "Okay. I'll go up and take photos. I'll send them to you in five minutes."

Calling out to Stella this time, he said, "I'm sorry. I'll be back in a few moments."

She heard him rush upstairs.

Stella had a feeling all this photography might take longer than five minutes. It sounded as if this client was demanding quite a few details. If only Graham had been able to give her the answers first, she thought, feeling stressed as she paced around the cluttered living room. Because now, she was stuck here until he'd wrapped up with his call, knowing he possessed important information that might be pivotal in solving the case.

Well, it had been frustrating every step of the way, so why should it change now? Stella decided wryly, knowing she needed patience. She wondered if she should rush over to Anthea's house and speak to her while Graham was busy. That would give him more time, but he might consider it rude, and in any case, she remembered he'd been about to head out to the store when she arrived.

She walked over to the dining room chair and sat down.

At that moment, her phone rang.

She answered it, wondering who was calling as the number was unfamiliar.

"Agent Fall? It's Kevin, Harriet's brother. I'm calling with the information I said I'd provide."

"Oh, yes. Thank you for calling back," Stella said. Even though she'd already confirmed with Graham why he hadn't told her about the timing of the divorce, she reminded herself never to ignore a small detail.

She felt relieved that Graham was partially deaf because otherwise it could have been awkward to stand in his house, confirming these details. It felt like she'd been second-guessing him and she didn't want him to know. Not when he was about to helpfully provide her with information on Jay.

"They were divorced eleven years ago, as I thought, and he moved out at the end of February," Kevin explained.

"Thank you," Stella said.

"He moved to Delaware. He rented a home for a month or two, and I believe he bought it after that. We then lost touch with him completely."

Delaware? Stella felt surprised. She'd never known Graham lived there. She'd never thought to ask. Now, the name was ringing unwanted alarm bells.

"Which address?" she asked.

"The address was Thirty-four Mockingbird Avenue, in Lewes, Delaware," Henry said.

Stella felt ice cascade down her spine.

"Thirty-four Mockingbird Avenue? Are you sure?"

"Yes, that's the address we forwarded the mail to."

She could not believe it. Graham Haddow had been living directly opposite the home where the previous crime had taken place.

This was no coincidence.

An avalanche of emotions overwhelmed Stella. She stared down at the moving boxes feeling utterly shocked by the fact she'd missed this.

All this time, the murderer had been right in front of them. Right opposite the home of his victims. Hiding in plain sight. Just as he had the last time. Concealed behind a frail, friendly harmless persona that she now realized was no more than an act and a lie.

"Agent Fall? Are you there?"

"Yes. Thank you so much for your help, Kevin."

She disconnected. She couldn't speak to him a moment longer after hearing that bombshell.

But then, movement by the stairway alerted her.

"Don't move. If you move, if you touch your weapon, I will shoot."

It was a cold, hard voice. Graham was speaking in a tone she'd never heard him use before.

Stella froze.

Her heart started banging, fast and urgent.

That was another lie, she realized. Graham had not been deaf. He'd just convinced her he was, but in fact, his hearing must be sharp enough for him to have overheard her repeat his previous address, and to realize she'd been speaking to Kevin again.

Slowly, she turned her head and stared at him.

The ice-cold psychopath that had been hiding behind his bumbling, likeable front, stared back. His eyes were like chips of granite. His hands, holding the gun, were rock steady. None of the trembling and uncertainty she'd seen before was visible now.

"I will shoot," Graham said. "Put your hands in the air."

Stella calculated the distance. He was ten feet away. At that distance, he would most probably hit her. She couldn't run in time. And nor could she attack him.

He'd caught her off guard and now she was all out of options.

She'd never seen such blank, cold eyes.

She raised her hands.

"I'm sorry you spoke to Kevin again. I didn't think he still had that address, or that you'd end up contacting him. Now we're in a difficult situation."

He walked into the room, being careful to stay beyond her reach as he moved behind her.

"I actually liked you. I never meant for this to happen," he remarked casually.

She didn't dare turn her head, but followed him as far as she could with her eyes. Then she kept still. She simply couldn't risk doing anything different. Not with such a dangerous man who she knew for sure would have no inhibition to shoot.

Her heart accelerated as she felt the tug which meant he'd removed her service pistol from its holster.

"I'll take this while I figure out what to do with you," he said thoughtfully.

Still keeping his own gun aimed at her, he moved into her view again, shoving the pistol into his belt.

Her mind was reeling. She could not believe that he'd just disarmed her. He had taken her gun away. This mature, fragile, likeable, helpful man was actually a monster. The likeability had deceived her. So, too, had his fragility. He was moving differently now. Standing straighter. Looking much stronger. It was amazing, she thought numbly, how the stoop of his shoulders and the apologetic lowering of his head had given her the impression he was much smaller than he actually was. He was a big guy. Rangy, and probably five-ten. She'd felt a coordinated strength in the way he'd tugged her weapon out.

This man, this monster, took all his pleasure in living a lie, concealing who he was, identifying his next victims, and then, when he could no longer control himself, unleashing the killing spree.

Stella felt shocked to the core that she hadn't seen who she was. She'd thought of him as a father figure. Someone the community trusted. Everyone's sweet old dad. Sitting there in the living room with him over cookies and coffee, she'd felt so comfortable and at ease, as if she'd been living through a moment that might have happened with her own father if things had been different. She remembered how kind and caring he'd seemed. All a gleeful act that this psychopath had reveled in. He'd taken pleasure in fooling her, in playing the part of a harmless elder she would never suspect.

She felt paralyzed, not only by shock, but also by shame. How badly she'd slipped up. How easily her own weaknesses and vulnerabilities had allowed her to be fooled.

Now, she had no doubt she would pay the price.

He walked over and locked the front door. He stood, watching her, whistling a tune under his breath.

"Upstairs with you, I think," he demanded. "Go on. Up the stairs."

Her arms were starting to ache but she held them high as she ascended the stairs.

His footsteps tramped behind her.

Upstairs, Stella saw that Graham's home was a different world. Downstairs was the show home that fit with his personality. The quaint living room with shabby furniture, memorabilia she now knew would mean nothing to him, floral cups and saucers in the kitchen.

Upstairs, she saw his mind.

She walked into a huge, stark bedroom with a black-covered bed. Garish, disturbing art filled the walls. A painting of a woman with an arrow piercing her breast. A glowering devil's face in deep black and red. Weights and a gym machine. Graham was far from frail. The truth in this master bedroom filled Stella with a deep sense of coldness.

"Why did you choose them?" she asked. "The Taylors, I mean?"

In the unlikely event she made it out of here alive, she was sure as hell going to try and get a confession from him. Although even as she had the thought, she knew that if she got a confession, it would prove he never intended for her to leave alive.

"They fit my parameters," he said. He didn't sound conversational and friendly anymore, the way he had spoken to her before, as if confiding in his favorite niece. Rather, he seemed as if he was explaining something to a stranger.

"In what way?"

"Neighbors, close enough for me to observe them. And child-free. It can be challenging to find people who fit the right profile. I won't involve children as it's unfair. I believe they are innocent and shouldn't be subjected to death or fear. It's only as we get older that we all become corrupted." He smiled, as joyless an expression as Stella had ever seen.

"So you don't involve children?"

"Never," he agreed.

"You don't do them often? Your kills?"

"I don't allow myself to. Too often would mean people noticed. As it is, I've been able to commit the perfect crimes, until now. You obviously know about the couple in Delaware, because I remember you mentioning that case when you asked me to look through the Taylors' home. It shocked me you'd already drawn parallels. I made sure to be careful what I said to you as it was clear from the get-go you were a smart girl. I made sure to act helpless, too." He paused. "Before that, there was another you didn't pick up in Ohio. That was a single man."

Stella remembered the older case that the detectives had briefly referred to in the Delaware file.

"That must have been about seventeen years ago. My wife and I moved to a different neighborhood after that. I always move afterward. And going back further, the previous one was a woman on her own. That one was even before I was married, when I still lived in Kentucky," he remembered. "They arrested the wrong person for that, so I was free and clear."

"And the valuable items?"

"They throw police off the trail. I don't care if they get found or not. The mere fact they are taken makes people go off in the wrong direction. Apart from you."

He stared at her again.

"Like I said, I didn't wish you any harm. In fact, I liked you. I wish you'd stayed away. Because now, we have a problem."

His gaze intensified. She could see he was thinking hard.

Stella felt adrenaline boiling inside her. She absolutely had to take him down, but the problem was she was up against an adversary she'd seriously underestimated. She couldn't afford to make the same mistake again, or she would instantly die. But what could she do?

Perhaps she could jump him.

She tensed, ready to try, but before she could, he shook his head.

"Don't do it, Stella Fall. Don't try. Because in my mind, I already have plan A, and plan B. And I also have another plan, plan C. I can disappear. There are steps I can take, documents I have prepared. I guarantee you that if I shoot you now, I will be gone from the area before anyone realizes what has happened," he promised her.

CHAPTER TWENTY SEVEN

Could Graham really follow up on his coldly confident threat? Stella realized to her dismay that he could.

Gunshots were loud and startling but they were not easy to pinpoint in terms of direction. People were always confused by their direction. They would be disoriented and scared. They'd come out of their houses asking where the noise had come from. That would give Graham the perfect chance to say he'd take a drive to the next street and investigate. Stella didn't know how he could disappear but she was dismayed to find she believed him. He was cunning, intelligent, and had a very high ability to preplan. He could have alternative documents stashed away that he'd obtained sometime in the past.

And, after all, she reminded herself that her own father had managed to disappear without a trace. If he hadn't written to her mother, she'd never, ever have known any different.

Graham put her gun down. Stella noted exactly where it was. It was on the other side of the room, on a shelf. She needed to get to it, but she couldn't. Not now.

He stuck his own gun into his belt. Then he turned and locked the bedroom door and put the key in his pocket.

She watched him, her mind filling with dread.

"I'm going to beat you to death," he said, in a tone of quiet satisfaction.

"No, you're not," Stella hissed back.

He picked up something from the floor. It was a long, heavy-looking baseball bat. Without a doubt this was the same weapon he'd used to murder Diane Taylor.

Stella barely had time to prepare herself before he attacked, and even then she realized she could not be prepared.

He leaped toward her and swung the bat at her, lethally fast, and she only just managed to duck out of the way of its swishing arc. The bat exploded down onto the desk behind her. Splinters flew.

Graham swung it at her again and she jumped back, flattening herself against the wall. Stella looked around, desperate for a weapon that she could use to defend herself, or even to attack in turn, but there was nothing available. The room was so empty. The paintings were encased in light wooden frames. There was a massive lamp that was too big to use, and the weights were too heavy to be thrown.

She jackknifed out of the way again as he swung at her a third time. The tip of the bat grazed her arm.

Her options were narrowing fast.

She had to do something. Try to get it away. But the problem was he was swinging it fast and furiously, and with a lot of expertise. As his momentum built, Stella had the clear impression this man was working himself into a killing rage.

"Come here," he hissed. "You can't run forever."

He lunged at her, raising the bat as high as he could.

This time, Stella didn't wait for him to bring it down. She lunged forward and tackled him, getting in close, grabbing him so that he couldn't use it on her.

But to her dismay, she came up against a wall of iron-hard muscle. Graham wrenched her back. Stella fought back with all her strength, going for the gun. If she could get it, then she had won.

But with a vicious kick, Graham dislodged her, and Stella had to roll out of the way as the bat came down with another whooshing arc.

He was insanely strong. That would be because he was insane. He had gleefully hidden the super-fast, powerful side that allowed him to kill. He reveled in the act he put on, fooling the world while he committed unspeakable violence. Now, she could hear the adrenaline-fueled wildness in his voice.

"You're fast, Stella. Very fast. I like that. It's going to be fun killing you. What a treat it will be, to get another chance so soon. Don't worry. We have lots of time," Graham said. "I don't even mind if you try to fight back. Diane tried. She didn't get far but I admired how even while I was killing her, she was trying to kick me away. At first," he added thoughtfully.

He whirled the bat at her again and this time it caught her a glancing blow on the shoulder and she yelled in pain. She'd hoped to try and grab it but now her whole arm was numb.

Stella scrambled over the bed, desperate to put some distance between them until she got feeling back in her right arm, and found herself near the window.

Calling for help might work. She tried to yank the window up with her left hand, thinking she could shout through the gap, or even jump out of it. She was willing to take the drop into a soft flower bed over being trapped in this room with this man.

But the window wouldn't budge.

"I fixed the latch," Graham laughed breathlessly. "I've thought of everything. I really have. We have all the time in the world now, you and I."

"Help!" Stella bashed on the window. It wasn't a loud noise, but possibly someone might notice.

"Stop that," he hissed, angry now. Again, she had to leap aside. She could see he was getting frustrated that she was evading him. He wanted violence, and was becoming hungry for it. She wasn't allowing him that. Just now, she guessed, he would give up on trying to beat her and he would use the gun. He'd kill her with it, or else disable her. Shoot her in the stomach and then come in again with the bat. Her time was running out.

A last-ditch solution occurred to her as she glanced at his weights in the corner.

"Stella Fall, Stella Fall," Graham chanted. He'd gotten over his anger and was back in his evilly confident mindset. "You'll be the first FBI agent I've ever killed. The first who's even gotten close. I wonder if they'll ever catch up with me. I doubt it. Because I have my exit plan. In fact, I've been looking forward to it. A new name, new identity. A fresh start."

Stella wasn't listening to him. Instead, drawing a deep breath, knowing the movement would open her up to attack, she dived forward and grabbed the closest dumbbell.

It was a dead weight in her left hand and her muscles screamed as she hauled it up. It was too big and clumsy to hurt him with, but that wasn't her plan.

She turned, and as hard as she could, she flung it against the window glass.

The glass exploded outward, and Graham's cry of rage went with it. The dumbbell arced through the shattered gap and a moment later, thudded dully into the flower bed below.

"Help!" Stella screamed at the top of her voice. "Help! Somebody, come and help me! Anthea! Roger!"

As she had feared, her actions had put a stop to the games. Graham pulled the gun out of his belt. He looked insane with rage.

"Get away! Get away from there, now! I am not going down for you. I am not!"

The gun was pointing at her, the muzzle black and deadly.

"The smashed window is a giveaway," she pointed out. Every moment she could delay him would work in her favor.

"Not if I shoot you quick enough," he retorted. "If I do, I can still get away myself. So it's time now. It's time, Stella."

But at that moment, there was a loud knock on the front door.

Stella didn't dare take her eyes off Graham but she saw his whole body tense. The confidence had gone from his face. Now, he looked trapped.

"Graham? Are you okay?" a voice called out. "I heard a smashing sound, and as if someone was shouting."

"Help!" Stella screamed again.

"Who's that?" the woman called, now sounding frightened.

It was Anthea, the friendly neighbor, the one Stella had come here to interview.

Graham hesitated, looking stressed and wild-eyed.

He couldn't shoot her now, Stella realized. Not with Anthea downstairs, at the door, waiting for him to answer. Not with the window smashed. Nobody could explain away such a close gunshot. And this curveball had confused him. He might have a sharp, intelligent mind, but he couldn't cope with this sudden derailment of his plans.

Stella knew this was her only chance and she had to take it.

She had to attack him now. While he was in shock, the same way she'd been earlier.

He was bigger and stronger but she had two major advantages. The first one was that she could use her voice and keep screaming.

Yelling at the top of her voice, "Help! Help me!" Stella leaped across the bed at him. He didn't shoot. He couldn't. Not when Anthea was calling again, "Graham, are you there?"

He swore violently as she grabbed the gun and struggled for possession of it, but she'd caught him by surprise. Stella managed to wrestle the gun away. It dropped to the floor. She would have liked to grab it, but without a second to spare, she had to make do with kicking it across the room.

With a hiss of rage, Graham launched himself at her, and finally, they were in hand-to-hand combat.

He was bigger and stronger than her, and had all the power of madness, but Stella hoped her second advantage lay in the fact that he would never have learned to fight.

He'd never had to. He'd always had the jump on his victims. Now, face to face with him, she knew her only chance would be to attack, as savagely as she could, and hope he couldn't defend himself adequately.

Ducking under his grasping hands, she slammed her left fist into his jaw with all her strength. He grunted and his head shot back, banging against the wall. Stella followed up with a chop to his neck so that he convulsed violently, choking and coughing.

"Help!" she screamed again, and heard Anthea's horrified shout back.

"What is going on? Graham, are you there? I'm calling the police!"

"Call nine-one-one! Now!" Stella screamed.

Graham kicked out at her and got her in the shin. She staggered, her leg on fire, but managed to keep on her feet as he lunged at her. She caught the punch that was headed for her solar plexus. She grabbed his arm and twisted it until she heard him let out a shrill cry of agony.

Stella knew what she had to do. She forced him around. Grabbed a handful of his gray hair. Slammed his face into the wall as hard as she could. He was flailing now, sobbing. She heard pain in his voice, and fear, too. He knew what was coming.

Slamming his head against the wall a second time, she felt him stagger, and knew the impact had stunned him.

She tugged at her belt and finally, her right arm cooperated enough for her to get the cuffs off their clip. She snapped them around one of his wrists. A moment later, she managed to haul his other hand behind him and got it cuffed, too. For good measure, she kicked his knees out from under him and watched as he sprawled face-first onto the ground.

She was breathing so hard it was coming out in sobs. She felt nauseous, traumatized beyond belief at what had played out in this room. The fight had left her feeling weak and battered and emotionally spent.

Quickly, she collected her gun from the shelf and picked up his as well.

Then she jammed her hand into Graham's pocket and took out the bedroom key. She unlocked the bedroom door and opened it, still holding her gun in her other hand, glancing back at Graham, who was flailing on the floor, groaning as he tried to sit up.

"Anthea, it's Stella Fall," she called.

"What?" Anthea shouted back, incredulously. "What happened up there?"

“Graham attacked me. He’s the killer. I’ve got him handcuffed now. I’ll come downstairs when the police arrive.”

“I don’t believe this,” she heard Anthea say in a shaky voice that was now coming from outside the window. She guessed the neighbor was looking up at the smashed glass.

Even though Graham was handcuffed, she didn’t dare to turn her back on him. Not even to go and convince Anthea she was telling the truth. That conversation could wait.

He struggled to his knees, but he wasn’t speaking. Staring at the wall, he was breathing harshly and spitting blood. She didn’t trust him, though. Handcuffed or not, dazed or not, Stella wasn’t going to lower the gun or move from the doorway until she heard the police arrive.

She knew that the evidence against him would now be overwhelming. No more lives would be destroyed by this evil monster, who had murdered for the sheer pleasure of it. Stella was certain he’d spend all his remaining years in jail.

Now, if only she could get the Marshalls in there with him, she thought, remembering her predicament with a shiver.

CHAPTER TWENTY EIGHT

When Stella walked along the corridor to Roth's office, feeling shredded and aching all over after her ordeal, the first person she saw was Maxwell. Looking anxious, he was waiting at the door, and hurried toward her as soon as he saw her.

"Fall," he said. "I just heard what happened."

To her surprise, he didn't look pleased the case was solved. Instead, he looked devastated.

"Yes. We solved it. And just in time. Graham was preparing to move. If I hadn't gone back there, we would probably never have caught him in time. He would have disappeared and been someone else's likeable, trustworthy neighbor until he murdered them."

She still felt sickened by the evil in his psyche.

"I know. That's all good. But Fall, I wasn't there for you! I can't believe you had to face that on your own! I mean, I heard all the details when you called them in, and they were horrific. He went after you with a baseball bat and a gun, and you had to smash a window to call for help."

"I underestimated him," Stella said.

The words tasted bitter as she uttered them. Humiliation filled her that she hadn't seen past his carefully constructed persona. After all, this was her area of expertise. She had done her master's thesis on people like him, and still she hadn't realized.

She'd been thoroughly, and far too easily, fooled.

"It was a lesson to me," she said, her voice harsh. "I was completely taken in. I didn't think he was a killer. This has taught me never to trust anyone who's a potential suspect in a murder. Even if they act weak and frail. I will not make the same mistake again. This was a brutal lesson to learn."

Clem had warned her to watch out for hidden evil and she hadn't seen where it was lurking.

Stella felt even more distressed that he'd preyed on her own vulnerability, too. She had allowed him, for a brief while, to fill the space inside her—that lonely space that longed for the calm, comforting father figure who had been torn away from her.

By another psychopath, Stella remembered, forcing back the sudden pang of loss she felt.

"But I should have been there for you. As your partner. Been there with you!"

She realized Maxwell was as angry with himself as she was with herself. The difference was that he hadn't misjudged anything, or made a mistake, like she had.

"You were there for me. Every step of the way. And at the time when this happened, you were just doing your job," she reminded him. "You were doing exactly what we discussed. If anyone should have realized who Graham was, it was me. I was the one who didn't see what I should have picked up. If I'd been smarter, I would have asked you to come with me."

"Unreal that such a person can hide behind a harmless front." Maxwell shook his head.

"I know. It's one of the most disturbing things I've ever had to experience. But I was listening to my own preconceptions and believing my judgment was right. This has taught me not to do that. I wasn't handling my interactions with him the way I should have. I hope I am never so naïve again."

"I was fooled by him, too. I wish I'd done more to help." Maxwell still looked angry with himself.

"At least the case is solved now," Stella said.

"Roth's pleased. He called me just now. He's in a meeting in D.C. and will be back tomorrow. But he's delighted it was solved so fast and he commended us both."

"That's good." Roth's praise was never given lightly and Stella felt a little of the heaviness inside her lift.

"I've signed off some of the paperwork already. There'll be more to do, but it won't be ready until tomorrow. So, if you're done here, shall we head home?" Maxwell asked.

"Yes. Let's go."

Home was not a comforting word at this time, after what had happened to her last time she'd gotten back. In fact, Stella felt uneasy all over again about having to return to her own space. Her apartment was only as safe as its strongest locks, and her enemies knew where to find her.

The only thing that gave Stella a shred of comfort as she walked out of the office with Maxwell, was that by now, Viv would have handed those documents to the police and the wheels had hopefully been set in motion. With any luck, her sleepless nights were numbered, because surely an arrest would soon be made.

Maxwell was clearly also thinking along those lines.

"Are you going to be safe?" he asked again. "Especially after what happened to you yesterday?"

"I'll be fine." Stella gave him her standard response. She could see he didn't buy it this time.

They walked out of the building and when they were outside, Maxwell gently took her arm and spoke in a low voice.

"There's something I need to tell you," he said.

"What?" Stella couldn't help it. Immediately, she felt nervous as she turned to face him.

"About Brigitte," he said, and his wife's name twisted her stomach instantly.

"What about her?" she asked.

"I'm meeting with her now. I set it up this morning and messaged her an hour ago to confirm the time, once I knew the case was wrapping up."

"What for?" Stella asked. Maxwell looked stern and resolute.

"She doesn't know yet, but I am getting a restraining order against her. I have already called my lawyer. I don't want her threatening you or me any longer."

"Oh, no." Stella realized Maxwell must have had much more on his plate than he had admitted to during their investigation.

"She's threatened harm to me and you. I can't risk her interfering any longer. I don't know what she's capable of. But I'm going to handle it in a positive way. I'm going to discuss all the options with her. I'm going to suggest she goes on an overseas vacation, takes time out to think this through. Maybe even relocates somewhere different. I'm going to support and help her all I can. I'll pay for her travels. I'll set her up wherever she wants to be."

"You think she'll agree?" Stella asked, feeling doubtful.

"That's what we're going to have to talk about," Maxwell said. "I don't know if she will agree. I have a feeling she might resist. But I am not giving her the choice. The restraining order will be enforced, regardless, and based on that, she will have to decide how far away from us she wants to be. She cannot compromise my life, and my job, and your life, and your safety."

He ticked the points off on his fingers as he spoke.

"That's going to be a tough meeting," Stella said. "I'll take the unmarked and drive home on my own."

She felt relieved and grateful that Maxwell was finally addressing the issues that had been hanging over him for so long.

"It is going to be tough. But it needs to be done. Enough's enough," Maxwell said. "And now, we'd better get going."

"We'd better," Stella said, and headed for her car.

As she walked to the unmarked, she felt huge respect that he was doing such a thing. Maxwell had to put a stop to it because the only other alternative was going to be that her behavior escalated.

The only problem was that she didn't rate Maxwell's chances. She had a feeling Brigitte was going to fight back, and hard.

As she climbed into her car, Stella's thoughts veered back to her own situation. Maxwell was doing what he could to address his problems. But she had no idea where things stood with Viv and the Marshalls. Why hadn't Viv called her yet?

Sitting inside the unmarked, unable to wait a moment longer, Stella dialed Viv's number. The call connected and rang and she felt a small, early blip of relief because Viv's phone was turned on. That had to be good, right? Turned off would be bad.

But, as it rang and rang unanswered, Stella felt the knot of tension tighten painfully inside her. It was unthinkable that Viv would not have updated Stella. Of course she would have, as soon as she could. But there hadn't been a message. Every time Stella had checked her phone during the course of the day, she'd hoped she might see a brief text, just letting Stella know that Viv was all right.

There had been nothing. She was now fearing that things were not all right and that something had gone terribly wrong.

What could she do?

Remembering Clem's advice on asking for help, Stella decided that she now needed to bring in the big guns, and ask Roth if the FBI could track Viv's phone. She was sure Roth would agree because after all, this was not just a personal problem but something that was affecting the safety of one of his staff.

If Viv hadn't called back or wasn't picking up by the time she got home, Stella resolved to start the search immediately.

CHAPTER TWENTY NINE

Maxwell glanced back in concern at Fall before getting into his car. There was something bothering her. That was freaking him out. And she wasn't telling him what it was. That was concerning him even more, because it meant it was serious.

Issues that were serious with Fall could affect her safety. He'd already seen that. She'd managed to get on the wrong side of some evil and powerful people. And now, she'd also managed to get on the wrong side of Brigitte.

Brigitte wasn't as wealthy and powerful as the Marshalls, but Maxwell had no illusions about her capacity to do damage. In the past, when she'd been at her most unhinged during their marriage, she'd physically attacked him. It wasn't something he'd ever mentioned since. He'd found it deeply distressing in a visceral way.

Her strength had been astounding. She'd attacked with no inhibition, scratching and clawing. She'd grabbed a knife and he remembered with a sick feeling how dangerous, how precarious, that entire situation had been for a moment.

He'd managed to grab her wrists and get the knife away. Still holding her, not daring to let go, he'd talked her down.

It had taken two hours and Maxwell never, ever wanted to think of that time again. The time he'd seen the other side of his wife. Who she could be.

After two hours she'd calmed down enough for him to drive her to the emergency room, where they'd administered a sedative. The next day, she'd been tearful and apologetic and had agreed to go back to the shrink to get her meds adjusted.

The point was, Maxwell thought heavily, that the damage Brigitte could have done would have been irreparable. He remembered only too well how his wrists had ached and burned from holding her back. How her screams had literally battered him. He'd had a blinding headache afterward. If she'd gotten to him with the knife, with her emotions so haywire and self-control nonexistent, Maxwell knew for sure she would have done serious harm.

It scared him beyond belief that the woman he'd loved, married, and trusted had changed so much. Or rather, had changed back to who she always was. It was beyond sad, because he knew she wouldn't have chosen to be that way if she'd had a choice.

Maxwell wished he could tell Fall his feelings. Losing her for a couple of months had proven to him how much she meant to him. He couldn't mess up again and now had to take steps to change his life, close up and end up what was toxic, and move on.

He and Brigitte had agreed to meet at Papas, an Italian restaurant that was two blocks away from the FBI offices. She'd said she would go there immediately when he had called her before leaving the office.

Maxwell drove straight there. He'd chosen Papas because it had a quiet upstairs section where he'd reserved a table. He hoped that being in a public place would mean things didn't get too out of hand during their discussion. Brigitte only unleashed her worst side when they were alone together.

He parked outside the restaurant, climbed out, and walked in, nodding a greeting to the manager.

"I have a reservation," he said. He headed upstairs.

When he reached the upstairs section, with its white-covered tablecloths and muted lighting, he stared in surprise. There was only one couple there in the corner, busy accepting a drinks order. There was nobody else in the restaurant's upper level at all.

Feeling confused, Maxwell turned away from the waiter, who was already approaching with menus. He went back downstairs and looked around. Brigitte had clearly told him she would go to the restaurant and be waiting. He'd told her upstairs, but maybe she'd missed that part of the conversation.

The downstairs section was busier and bigger. He walked through it, checking every table.

Brigitte wasn't there.

Now feeling inwardly frantic, Maxwell went outside to call her. There was no reason why she should not be here, other than something must have gone wrong. What had happened? Had she been delayed, had she had a crash or gotten into a road rage incident?

He called her number and waited.

The phone rang and rang until it went through to voicemail.

Maxwell left her a message. Then he sent her a text, noticing she'd last checked her messages five minutes ago.

If she'd read her messages, that meant she was okay. There wasn't a crisis, she hadn't lost her phone, hadn't been in a crash.

But she wasn't here. She hadn't arrived for this very important meeting where he had planned to discuss their future, lay his cards on the table, and present her with an ultimatum.

Had she known?

The thought chilled Maxwell. Brigitte could well have guessed why Maxwell wanted to meet her. In fact, now he thought about it, there was no other reasonable explanation for why he would suddenly have wanted to get together at a restaurant.

"Damn, damn," he muttered, staring left and right into the darkened street, looking for any sign of her or her car.

She'd realized where this was going and because of that, she had decided not to be here. And she'd done so at the last minute. She had played along, agreed to meet, said she'd go to the venue, and then she hadn't arrived.

This was totally and utterly deliberate, and the burning question now was: where was she?

Had she used this time, when she knew that Maxwell would be here, to go somewhere else? To try and destroy the person she perceived as a threat?

Maxwell breathed fast as he remembered how he'd told her the case was solved and he'd be on his way. It would not have taken a huge leap of logic to deduce that if the case was over, both he and his partner would be heading home.

He needed to get to Fall as soon as he could.

If Brigitte reached her first, this had the potential to turn into a huge disaster.

CHAPTER THIRTY

Stella drove into her apartment's basement parking garage and looked around cautiously before she got out. She felt a faint but distinct sense of threat. She scanned all the shadows. Who was there, watching?

What had happened to Viv?

She couldn't shake the strong feeling that someone was watching her. She swung around, staring into the basement's gloom.

Although she couldn't see anyone, she knew that did not mean nobody was there. Somehow, she was sure unfriendly eyes were on her, and her movements were being monitored.

If you don't kill it, it'll get even angrier!

Apropos of nothing, that phrase surfaced in her mind. She couldn't remember where she'd heard it or what the original circumstances behind it had been. It must have been back in her school days, and referring to a dangerous insect or animal. But the meaning chilled her now. If the Marshalls knew she and Viv had tried to bring them down and hadn't succeeded, their fury would know no bounds.

At any rate, there seemed to be nobody in the basement. She couldn't hear or see anyone and had no idea why she'd had such a cold, sharp instinct. She trudged to the stairs and opened the door warily.

The stairwell was clear. She paused, listening. There were no unusual sounds. She had no sense that anyone might be waiting.

Should she take the elevator? she wondered. But that would be giving in to her fear.

At that moment, her phone buzzed. She had an incoming message.

To her massive relief, she saw it was from Viv.

That incoming message made her feel weak at the knees. Viv had texted at last. She must be all right, but had everything gone as planned?

Grabbing the phone, Stella anxiously read the message. And then she frowned. This didn't make sense at all. Not at all!

"Stop bullying me. I won't be manipulated by you anymore and I'm not doing what you have been asking me to. It's not legal and will have repercussions. Leave me out of this. And I'm not going to give you

money so stop trying to make me. Leave the entire situation alone, Stella."

"What is this?" Stella whispered, horrified.

It was as if Viv had gone mad. Had she meant to send this strange, angry message to someone else? Were there other things going on in her life? But she'd addressed Stella by name. So it had to be meant for her.

Stella simply couldn't understand it. It felt as if her entire reality had been turned upside down. With a terrible lurch of her heart, she wondered whether Viv had been on the Marshalls' side the whole time, and had just been stringing Stella along.

Then she told herself to think logically. Viv's behavior could no way have been an act.

She'd been in danger. Stella had not imagined her stress and terror. She'd even missed the charity event and kept out of the public eye.

Maybe she still was. That was it. Light dawned. This message must be a cover.

Viv must suspect that someone had seen them together or known they had been in communication. So the message had been sent to throw whoever it was off the trail. Perhaps she thought one of the Marshalls might get hold of her phone.

But by now the key players in this whole scenario should be in jail.

Maybe they weren't, though. Maybe one of Cecilia's children had asked to meet with Viv and she wanted to avert suspicion.

There must be a reason, but having received this message, Stella knew she couldn't keep trying to contact Viv. Any further calls to her after this would be pointless and would destroy the scenario created by this message.

She'd have to wait for Viv to contact her and explain. Stella was sure she'd find a way to do so, perhaps using a different number. And at least she knew that she was alive and well. That was a relief.

So, for now, Stella had to put this aside and focus on her own safety. Especially since this message meant that there was still a need to be very aware.

She ascended the stairs, taking her time. Listening out before she reached every landing. It seemed the coast was clear. She reached the fifth floor and let out a breath of relief as she pushed the door open. At least she had survived the stairs. Life was already a hundred percent better than it had been the previous time she'd gotten home, she thought, trying to lighten her sense of threat with some humor.

She walked down the corridor.

And then tensed as, ahead of her, she heard the fast thudding of footsteps and a woman's panicked cry.

Stella shrank back against the rail, her heart accelerating, her hand dropping to her gun as the footsteps rounded the corner.

What was happening?

The footsteps stormed toward her and she waited, heart hammering, her muscles tensing, ready to act.

"Damn, I'm so late! So late!" the voice cried out again as the woman came into view, a thirty-something-year-old whom she'd seen a few times before, visiting the apartment at the end of the row.

"So late! And it's going to take twenty minutes to get to the venue!" She rushed past Stella with a clatter of heels, checking her phone as she ran. She didn't even notice Stella as she skidded to a stop outside the elevator. A moment later Stella heard it ping.

She let out a deep breath.

So much for that. It had been a normal person. Just a normal person in a rush. Nothing more. Not this time, anyway.

Her apartment door was locked. Everything looked as it had when she had left. She was home and could now make sure that her place was secured for the night, and wait for Viv to get hold of her with any news.

Stella unlocked her apartment door.

She opened it.

And instantly, she saw it.

She gasped a huge breath of air and then clapped her hand over her mouth so it didn't erupt in a scream.

Viv was there, in her apartment.

She was sprawled on the two-seater couch. There was a bloody dent in her forehead. Her eyes were wide open. Undoubtedly, she was dead.

Stella recoiled, clutching the doorframe, feeling panic explode inside her as she took in the awful scene. Someone had gotten into her private space. They'd killed Viv and they'd left her there. In her own apartment!

Horrified, she rushed over to Viv, grabbing her limp wrist, checking for a pulse, hearing her own sobs frantic in the otherwise silent apartment.

Viv. This couldn't be. Stella felt an agonizing sense of loss at the death of the brave, strong, funny, courageous woman who'd been in Stella's corner and whom she'd ended up liking and admiring. Grief surged inside her as she checked her pulse, even though she knew already it was a formality.

No pulse. Viv's wrist was cool, but not cold. Rigor mortis had not set in. This must have happened recently.

Very recently, Stella thought with a sense of utter doom as she began joining the dots.

The message to Stella had told a clear story. It had illustrated a serious problem between her and Viv.

Ice washed down her spine as she realized Viv had not sent that message. Somebody else had. Someone who had wanted to lay a strong foundation for a scenario where Stella herself would look guilty.

What would the police think after reading that message, and seeing the body here? They would think there had been bad blood between them and that Stella had been pushing Viv to do something illegal that she was refusing to.

Viv had ended up here and they had fought. Stella had demanded money and ended up killing her. That was the picture they'd painted.

Killed her? With what?

Stella's eyes fell on the fire extinguisher that had been in its usual place in her apartment's kitchenette.

It was not in its place now. It was lying on the living room floor. The red base was dented, and darkened with blood.

There was her story. Laid out from start to finish. She'd been angry with Viv and had grabbed the closest weapon at hand, and attacked her with it.

This was the scheme that would land her in jail. Not forever, but for long enough that the Marshalls could easily dispose of her. With the right connections, which they had, it was easy to kill someone in jail, whether it ended up looking like outright murder, a fight, or a suicide.

"No, no, no!" Stella heard herself whispering.

They had thought this through so carefully, so cunningly, that she now felt completely checkmated. There was no escape route in this detailed scenario. She was sure Viv's car was parked nearby with her phone inside, showing that she'd arrived here and then come storming up to wait for Stella. She was sure every step of the way, the guilt could be traced back to her.

How could she fight it? How?

The enormity of their evil blindsided her and for a moment, she couldn't think coherently.

But she knew she would not have much time. They would send the police in as soon as they could. Someone, Kathy perhaps, would make a call.

"*I was visiting a friend and heard two women fighting. It sounded serious. One was screaming for her life. Please come quickly.*"

That was what they would do. This was the end game she could expect in a few short minutes.

And then she whirled around as loud, running footsteps sounded behind her.

She rushed back to the apartment door, and to her utter consternation, found herself face to face with Maxwell.

"Stella! Are you okay? I couldn't get hold of Brigitte and I was worried she had come here. She messaged me as I was on my way up here, saying she'd changed her mind about our meeting, but I still don't trust her."

"She didn't come here. But someone else did," Stella said, seeing Maxwell's face change, anxiety hardening his features as he took in her tear-stained, sheet-white face. "Maxwell, I've been framed. Viv, who was helping me fight the Marshalls, is here, and she's dead."

"What?" Staring past her, Maxwell took in the awful sight.

"Oh, hell, Stella."

He wasn't even calling her Fall anymore, her mind dimly registered. The distance between them was forgotten now, swept aside by this crisis.

"You don't know anything? Didn't see?" Maxwell asked.

"I just got back! They sent me a message from her phone as I arrived in the basement. It's highly incriminating. It suggests I was pressuring her for something illegal and for money. It lays the foundation for us to have fought. And they killed her with my fire extinguisher."

"We can get past this. We must get past it. We'll be able to prove you innocent," Maxwell insisted.

From outside, Stella heard the blare of sirens. She knew the cars were heading down Main Street. They were only minutes away.

"They've already called the cops. That's their plan, that's what they constructed this scenario for. They must have someone in the prison system who's been paid to get rid of me. Whether it happens in the precinct jail or in the prison, they have made a plan to kill me and this is why they did this. They just need me in there for long enough to get it done. If I get arrested, I won't get out. I am certain I will die."

"Stella—jeez. What can we do? What can I do?" Maxwell grasped her hand. His fingers felt cold. His eyes were blazing.

She looked into them as she gave the unthinkable decision.

"There are only two alternatives. You can arrest me, as you should do, based on this evidence, and your mandate as an officer of the law. Or you can help me. And helping me means assisting a fugitive, because that's what I'll have to be. I'm going to have to run. Now. There's no other choice."

She waited, feeling as if her entire future pivoted on the next few moments, to see what Maxwell would say.

A NEW SERIES!

NOW AVAILABLE!

<u>WITHOUT MERCY</u>
(A Dakota Steele FBI Suspense Thriller —Book 1)

MMA champ-turned-FBI Special Agent and BAU specialist Dakota Steele is as tough as they come—and as brilliant, too, able to crack serial killers that no one else can. But this new case is unlike anything she's seen, and Dakota, weighed down by the demons of her own past, may have just reached her breaking point.

"The plot has many twists and turns, but it is the ending, which I did not see coming at all, that totally defines this book as one of the most riveting that I have read in years."
—Reader review for Not Like Us

WITHOUT MERCY is the debut novel of a brand new series by critically-acclaimed and #1 bestselling mystery and suspense author Ava Strong.

Dakota's last case broke her, driving her to quit the FBI and return to the hard streets of her South Dakota hometown. She is weighed down by a lifetime of fighting, and by the demons of her dark past: her missing sister who vanished when Dakota was a teenager. Her estranged father, who she still can't bring herself to speak to.

The killer she let get away.

Dakota has hit her low point.

Only the most desperate case—and the tough love of her partner—can lure her back.

Victims are disappearing along empty stretches of desert highway, with no witnesses. The landscape is desolate, the people tough and dangerous. And the police are stumped.

Time is running out before the next victim is taken, and it's up to Dakota to connect the dots.

Can Dakota stop him in time?

Or will her own demons take her for good?

A complex psychological crime thriller full of twists and turns and packed with heart-pounding suspense, the DAKOTA STEELE mystery series will make you fall in love with a brilliant new female protagonist and keep you turning pages late into the night.

Books #2 and #3 in the series—WITHOUT REMORSE and WITHOUT A PAST—are now also available.

Ava Strong

Debut author Ava Strong is author of the REMI LAURENT mystery series, comprising six books (and counting); of the ILSE BECK mystery series, comprising seven books (and counting); of the STELLA FALL psychological suspense thriller series, comprising six books (and counting); and of the DAKOTA STEELE FBI Suspense thriller series, comprising three books (and counting).

An avid reader and lifelong fan of the mystery and thriller genres, Ava loves to hear from you, so please feel free to visit www.avastrongauthor.com to learn more and stay in touch.

BOOKS BY AVA STRONG

REMI LAURENT FBI SUSPENSE THRILLER
THE DEATH CODE (Book #1)
THE MURDER CODE (Book #2)
THE MALICE CODE (Book #3)
THE VENGEANCE CODE (Book #4)
THE DECEPTION CODE (Book #5)
THE SEDUCTION CODE (Book #6)

ILSE BECK FBI SUSPENSE THRILLER
NOT LIKE US (Book #1)
NOT LIKE HE SEEMED (Book #2)
NOT LIKE YESTERDAY (Book #3)
NOT LIKE THIS (Book #4)
NOT LIKE SHE THOUGHT (Book #5)
NOT LIKE BEFORE (Book #6)
NOT LIKE NORMAL (Book #7)

STELLA FALL PSYCHOLOGICAL SUSPENSE THRILLER
HIS OTHER WIFE (Book #1)
HIS OTHER LIE (Book #2)
HIS OTHER SECRET (Book #3)
HIS OTHER MISTRESS (Book #4)
HIS OTHER LIFE (Book #5)
HIS OTHER TRUTH (Book #6)

DAKOTA STEELE FBI SUSPENSE THRILLER
WITHOUT MERCY (Book #1)
WITHOUT REMORSE (Book #2)
WITHOUT A PAST (Book #3)

www.ingramcontent.com/pod-product-compliance
Lightning Source LLC
Chambersburg PA
CBHW030616310726
48979CB00003B/741

* 9 7 8 1 0 9 4 3 9 4 4 6 6 *